The Lawyer's Chambers

and other stories

Lowell B. Komie

SWORDFISH
CHICAGO

In 1983, nine of Lowell Komie's stories were published in a paperback edition entitled *The Judge's Chambers* by the American Bar Association, the first time in its history that the American Bar Association published a collection of fiction.

In 1987, thirteen of his stories were published by a publisher in Chicago both in paperback and hardcover in a collection known as *The Judge's Chambers and Other Stories.*

In 1994, this collection of seventeen stories was published by Swordfish/Chicago. These are seventeen new stories, not previously collected with the exception of "Podhoretz Revisited" which appeared in the 1987 collection.

"The Honorable Alicia Beauchamp," "Solo," "The Ice Horse," "Spring," "Justine," and "Podhoretz Revisited" were published in *Student Lawyer:* the magazine of the law student division of the American Bar Association. "A Woman in Prague", "A Woman in Warsaw" and "A Man in Montreal" were published in the *Chicago Tribune Magazine,* "Origami Aeroplane" in *Harper's,* "Ash" and "Investiture" in the *Chicago Bar Record,* "The Kisses of Fabricant" in *Chicago Magazine,* and "The Emerald Bracelet" in *Chicago Monthly.* "Casimir Zymak" was published in Karamu, Eastern Illinois University, and "Burak" by the American Bar Association. "The Pool Party" has never been previously published.

Published in 1994 by Swordfish/Chicago
155 North Michigan Avenue
Chicago. Illinois 60601
Copyright © 1994 Lowell B. Komie
Printed and bound in the USA

Library of Congress Catalog Card Number: 94-92227

Komie, Lowell B.
    The Lawyer's Chambers and Other Stories

    1. Lawyers—Fiction   I. Title

ISBN: 0-9641957-0-4

For our family

Also with gratitude to
David Komie, John Fink, Norbert Blei, Ann Lee,
and Anna Leja, who helped produce this book
and to Catherine Zaccarine who designed it.

My appreciation to Sarah Hoban
and Miriam Krasno who edited
many of these stories.

And a special thank you to
Denis Gosselin.

Contents

The Lawyer's Chambers

The Hon. Alicia Beauchamp.................................3

Investiture...19

Solo 31

The Ice Horse 43

Ash 59

Casimir Zymak..73

The Emerald Bracelet 81

Spring..91

Justine 101

Podhoretz Revisited 121

Burak..129

The Writer's Chambers

A Woman in Prague..................................135

A Man in Montreal..................................143

Origami Aeroplane 153

The Pool Party......................................161

The Kisses of Fabricant............................177

A Woman in Warsaw 187

The
Lawyer's
Chambers

The Honorable Alicia Beauchamp

S HE WAS LIKE MEDUSA, her husband had said to her the year before the divorce. Except the snakes coiled around her head weren't visible. If a man was caught by her glance, ultimately she would turn him to stone. It was a remark she'd never forgotten.

After their divorce, she found herself avoiding men of her age; she preferred the company of older men. It wasn't as painful, and as she too grew older she was beginning to become more adroit at avoiding pain. Instead she covered herself with work. She was a judge in the District Court in Milwaukee. Alicia Beauchamp was the youngest judge in the district. She was thirty-six when she was appointed by President Bush. Her auburn hair was worn very short in back with a crown of an extravagant red feather cut that made her look almost like an alert, angry bird. Her eyes, though, were soft and easily filled with humor. She had a short nose, pale skin, delicate cheekbones, and a small mouth. She preferred dark shades of lipstick and she seemed, when you approached her bench, strangely beautiful to be enrobed in black. Black, though, was the color of justice, she soon learned, and now, after almost two years on the federal bench, her eyes, which had sparkled so easily into laughter, were no longer so easily animated.

This morning the clerk had called the first case: "United States of America vs. John Gakubiak, 90 C 126." The defendant and his attorney stepped forward. Her clerk handed the file up to her. She put her glasses on and looked at the file. The defendant, a short,

bald man of about forty-five, with a heavy face and nervous darting eyes, stood with his hands clasped behind his back. John
Gakubiak had been accused of counterfeiting government tax
refund checks throughout the country. He was a Milwaukee resi-
dent, and the government had flown in a special prosecutor team
from the Justice Department in Washington to handle the case. He
was being defended by a Milwaukee lawyer she knew slightly from
bar association functions.

"Good morning, Mr. Johnstone." She took off her glasses.

"Good morning, Your Honor."

"Good morning, sir," she nodded to the defendant.

"Where is the government," she asked, looking around the
courtroom.

"I'm sorry, Your Honor," Johnstone turned to look at the
lawyers seated in the courtroom. "I haven't seen them, but perhaps
Your Honor would pass the case and call it again."

"No, I think not. We'll just wait a few moments". She looked
at her watch. "It's 9:30. If they aren't here by 9:38, I'll send the
jury back for reassignment and we'll not go forward this morning.
So we'll wait several minutes." She looked up at the big clock on
the side of the wall and tapped her pen on her papers. Her mouth
had compressed into a thin line and all the color had drained from
her face.

There was no sound in the courtroom. None of the lawyers seated at the counsel tables spoke. Johnstone folded his hands and stood
silently in front of her, as did the defendant, his head was bowed.

"It's now 9:34, gentlemen. We'll wait another four minutes."
She looked at her watch again. The courtroom remained silent,
while the four minutes passed.

"It's now 9:38. Will the clerk please dismiss the jury and send
them back to the jury room for reassignment. Mr. Johnstone, can
we agree on another date for status without bringing down another
jury? Perhaps the 26th, at 9:30. Also, I'll entertain at that time a
motion for costs against the government for your appearance here
today. Call the next case."

"Central Chemical Consortium vs. The Omicron Corporation, 90 C 2312."

Another set of lawyers approached the bench. She quickly reached for the file. The government was always flying people in from Washington. Why did they need special counsel in *Gakubiak?* It wasn't that complicated. They could have handled the case in Milwaukee. Anyway, the Justice Department lawyers weren't going to keep her or her courtroom waiting. They would learn that she wasn't going to wait on them. She wasn't a handmaiden.

She looked down at the next group of lawyers. There were two women and two men, all smiling up at her. Did she recognize any of them? No, she didn't know them. The women looked familiar. She removed the briefs from the file. "I've looked over both parties' briefs in *Chemical Consortium.* The first thing I've noticed is that they both exceed fifteen pages, so I've automatically stricken them. You know that we don't permit briefs in excess of fifteen pages without court permission, and permission is seldom granted. I don't have to go into the reasons for this rule. We're inundated with briefs. The word is a misnomer because the legal profession is unaware of the concept of brevity. We'll continue this thirty days for ruling, each side to file new briefs within ten days. If the new filings exceed the court rule on brevity, there will be sanctions imposed against each side."

The lawyers looked at their feet. One young woman looked up at her and was about to say something, and finally said nothing.

The two women lawyers had looked so pale. Do I look that pale? Am I that exhausted? They must touch their faces with an expensive gray cosmetic. They both probably make more money than I do, two or three years out of law school. There was a poem of Yeats, "The Magi." "...gray-faced like..." No, "Now, as at all times, I can see in the mind's eye, in their stiff painted clothes, the pale unsatisfied ones..." She stood up. "There will be a five-minute recess." She quickly walked off the bench and back into her chambers.

She wasn't going to quote them Yeats. She needed a vacation. She was exhausted. She began every day at eight with pretrial conferences. She often worked in her chambers until 10 or 11. She'd met a man recently, a man from India, a professor of economics at Marquette, and they were supposed to see each other tonight, Friday night. She was going to take two days Monday, but there was a judicial convention on federal appellate practice in Madison Monday and Tuesday. She poured herself a cup of coffee and sat in the chair behind her desk.

Of course they all made more money than she did. Why should she delude herself? She *was* a handmaiden. She waited on corporations and their lawyers at their pleasure. Teams of young lawyers representing corporate clients would attend her status calls. The best young people in the profession were used by their firms to create unjustified billable hours. They spent endless hours in the firm libraries working until midnight, working on weekends, on Sundays, to bill more hours. She could always tell how much a male partner made, though, by looking at his shoes. If he wore loafers with tassels, he made more than $200,000. If he only had a razor cut, a chalk pinstripe suit, and no loafers with tassels, he made $150,000 to $200,000. With rings on their fingers and bells on their toes, these men weren't lawyers, they were corporate employees. She wasn't going to quote them Yeats; she'd save Yeats for herself. The firms were cutting back anyway and many of the young lawyers would be let go. Where would they go? Legal Aid? The federal defender's office? That's where they were needed but they couldn't afford to work there. Maybe she should quit and go to Ireland and visit Yeats's swans at Coole. She sipped her coffee and put her feet up on her side table. She was so tired of all this, the endless paper chain of gray-clothed lawyers, the criminal defendants in their orange jumpsuits—they never stopped coming. Every cocaine dealer and runner in the city was passing though her courtroom. The more people she sentenced, the more appeared. Maybe she should really resign. Federal judges in Miami were resigning. They simply got tired of always being immersed in the drug culture. Where would she go? Back to her firm? She could probably teach in law school. She'd like to teach young people. She could take a sabbatical and then come back and open her own office and take only cases that merited a lawyer. Maybe she'd fall in love with someone. There were too many maybes.

She zipped up her judge's robe and touched her hair and stared at herself in the mirror. She suddenly walked back into the courtroom, almost taking her clerk and the lawyers by surprise as she entered.

"Call the next case," she said.

She saw the two Justice Department lawyers enter the courtroom. They were wheeling a cart with stacks of files and paged law books. She didn't acknowledge them. The lead attorney shook his head at her as they sat down. They both had wet umbrellas.

"Is that it?" she asked the clerk.

"No, Your Honor, the government has appeared in *Gakubiak*."

"Call *Gakubiak*."

"United States of America vs. John Gakubiak, 90 C 126."

"Gentlemen."

"Good morning, Your Honor." They wheeled their cart close to the bench. "The United States is ready for trial," the lead attorney said. He had a bony, angular, thin face, with tiny, darting eyes behind thick rimless glasses. His accent was nasal and, he was about 33 and a real whiner.

"The United States is late for trial." She shot her hand out and looked at her watch. She wore a Minnie Mouse watch, and this morning Minnie was in good shape and smiling at her with her hands held at 10:00. "It's 10:00, Mr. Gibbons. The case was set for 9:30."

"Your Honor, the government apologizes for the delay. As you can see from our clothes and umbrellas, it's raining. We flew in from Washington this morning. We had difficulty getting a cab at the airport and got caught in traffic. We apologize to Your Honor. However, we are here and ready to go forward." His assistant, who was slight and blonde, about twenty-five, sniffed and stared at her.

"Also, Your Honor," Gibbons continued, "we have this morning, before we proceed with the trial, the government's motion *in limine*." Gibbons glanced at his junior who immediately handed him the motion.

"Mr. Gibbons, this is no time to file a motion *in limine*, on the day of the trial. You can't seek to limit introduction of evidence by the defendant on the day of the trial. He has to be given the opportunity to respond. I have to consider each exhibit you seek to bar. This can't be done on the day you pick the jury. You know that. I suggest that by appearing here a half hour late and seeking to file a motion *in limine*, with a jury waiting to be examined and impaneled, you show absolute disrespect for this court and its procedures, a lack of respect almost bordering on contempt."

"Your Honor," Gibbons began to whine, "I have no lack of respect for the court. The trial hasn't begun, the jury hasn't been picked, there are no jurors in the box, the government has a right to file a motion *in limine*, we are prepared to do so." He began to hand the motion to her clerk.

"Denied."

"You're denying the government the right to even file its motion?"

"Denied. Do you know what that means?"

"The government reserves the right to renew its motion and nevertheless is ready for trial."

"There will be no trial this morning, Mr. Gibbons. The defendant was here at 9:30 with his counsel. The case was called, the government was not here. The jury was waiting to be brought in for questioning and to be impaneled. We held the case for several minutes. No one from the government appeared."

"Your Honor, we are here now. We were unavoidably detained. I apologize to the court, but we are ready to go forward."

"Well, the government's case is not going forward today. Mr. Gakubiak has a bond for his appearance. The government will not be prejudiced. You were late, and my courtroom does not wait on the Government or on any litigant. The government does not have a special status in my courtroom. The case was continued to the 26th. The status call is now completed."

She stood. The clerk rapped her gavel. Judge Beauchamp walked out of the courtroom.

SHE TOOK OFF her robe, washed her hands and face, and sprayed her wrists with cologne. Gibbons was really an offensive man. She couldn't stand him. Her remark, though, about contempt wasn't justified. Still, he had absolutely no sense of courtesy or civility. She combed her hair. She couldn't call the chief judge and ask for another trial today because she'd have only the afternoon and then there would be the weekend and on Monday, the two-day conference.

She really didn't want to go to the conference. But she'd volunteered to speak. There were no women on the Court of Appeals in this circuit, no women, no blacks, no Asians, no Hispanics, only white males. She wanted to have this chance to confront them. To her it was just another male club. They'd overruled and remanded at least five of her cases since she'd been appointed. She had recused herself on three of them. It was a cute but deadly game, and she played it as well as they did. She was surprised they'd even invited her. The title of her speech was "Appellate Review or Appellate Apartheid?" If you're black or other minority in this circuit the review of your case on appeal will be by a panel of all-white male judges who are completely alien to your background and your culture. More than 90 per cent of the drug defendants are black or Hispanic and at least 25 per cent of her call involved drug cases. If you're a black woman in prison, you're up against the system alone and disadvantaged by gender as much as by skin color. When was the last time she'd taken an afternoon off? Two years ago? She should just go home and go for a walk through the park along the lake and then do some shopping. She was supposed to meet the professor tonight at six at the Art Museum.

She put on her coat, turned off her desk lamp and picked up the phone and called her clerk. "Madelyn, I'm taking the afternoon off. Don't fall over in shock. In fact, I won't be back until Wednesday morning because of the conference. If you have to reach me, leave a message on my machine at home. I'll beep it this afternoon at 2:30 and then at 11 on Saturday and 2 on each day I'm gone. Please also post a notice on the board in front of the courtroom about my absence. Judge Swenson will be the emergency judge while I'm gone."

SHE WAS AT the Art Museum early and went in to see some of the collection. She loved the three paintings of flowers by Emil Nolde, a German painter—this was a lovely place to wait for someone. She could see the lake framed in the huge glass window and sailboats heading out past the breakwater.

Then suddenly she saw him. He was standing in the corner of the gallery watching her. "You like Nolde, I see," he said to her.

"Yes, Nolde is marvelous. His flowers are almost translucent with light."

"Have you seen the Chagalls?" He reached out and touched her arm and led her to two Chagalls on the far wall. The large painting was of a man on a horse. The man wore a cape of flowers, the horse a bridle of flowers. The woman in the background held two babies. The smaller painting was of a bouquet of poppies.

"More flowers." He led her into another gallery where he showed her a large painting of a French peasant and a young girl, perhaps a grandfather and granddaughter, walking in the woods. The old man carried a large bundle of sticks on his back. The little girl had an angelic face and fine blonde hair and walked just ahead of him picking wild flowers.

"'Pere Jacques,'" he said, squinting at the painting. "Jules Bastien-Lepage, 1881. I think it's the most beautiful painting in the collection. The old woodcutter's face has the dignity of old age; his granddaughter looks like a young princess, standing in a field of flowers. She's such a beautiful child."

Neither of them spoke and as they stood together before the painting, she could feel a rush of longing, the scent and feel of desire for this man...his mouth, his eyes, the sound of his voice.

Later at the outdoor cafe at the old hotel on Wisconsin Avenue they talked. Rajiv Nair was a professor of economics and he was leaving for three months in Geneva where he was going to do a project for the United Nations on food distribution in Third World countries. He would attend the conference and stay and write a paper. He was from Bangalore in the south of India and was a widower. His wife had died of malaria five years ago, and his mother was caring for their child, a girl of seven, in New Delhi.

"And you, Alicia, what is your occupation?" he asked, ordering a cappuccino for both of them.

"I work for the government."

"What type of work do you do?"

"Well, it's mostly legal and administrative. It's very bureacratic."

"Government work is always bureaucratic." He stopped asking questions and looked around them. "Milwaukee is a beautiful city, no? I hate to leave it. It's very European and Old World. I love the buildings. They remind me of turn-of-the-century Vienna."

"How long will you be gone, Rajiv?" It was the first time she'd used his name.

"Three months."

"And then you'll return to Marquette?"

"Yes, to Marquette. I'm quite happy there. I miss my daughter and my mother, but I might fly to India to see them as long as I'm in Europe. It's a pity we've met just as I am leaving."

After they finished the cappuccinos, they went across the street to a bookstore she knew. She bought a book of Yeats, a small, beautifully illustrated edition. They walked back down Wisconsin Avenue to the lakefront and into the park and sat on a bench and watched the people in the park, bicyclists, joggers, people out walking their dogs. Afterwards he walked her back to her apartment. They stood under some trees, and he asked if he could see her tomorrow evening. "Yes, I would like to see you again, Rajiv." "I'll call you at five then," he said, touching her hand, and turned away without looking back.

That night she read some of Yeats and also Emily Dickinson
—"Hope is a thing with feathers." Woody Allen has written,
though, that "Hope is a thing without feathers." She smiled to herself and fell asleep in the chair in the living room, holding the
Dickinson poems and listening to Edith Piaf.

In the morning she walked along the lakefront and then had
coffee and a bagel at a hotel drugstore, read the paper and lingered
over breakfast. On weekdays she usually gulped down a cup of
black coffee in the kitchen and drove to the court building and her
morning court call. She never had time for breakfast. Even on the
weekends she usually spent Saturday mornings reading pre-sen-
tence reports and drafting preliminary orders in criminal cases.
Most of the cases involved narcotics. She had beeped her answering machine yesterday afternoon and there was nothing. This
morning when she called from the hotel coffee shop, her clerk had
left a message that the government had filed a motion in *Gakubiak*
for certification of an interlocutory appeal. They had noticed it for
Wednesday morning.

He came to pick her up at seven and they went to a play at the
Milwaukee Repertory Center. Afterwards they ate at a small
French restaurant he knew, and after dinner they returned to the
same park bench and sat watching the boats in the harbor. He put
his arm around her and she rested her head on his shoulder. She
felt completely relaxed and safe with this man.

When they walked back to the apartment, she asked him if he
would come up. She played her Piaf tape for him, and he looked at
the books on her bookshelf. There was nothing in her apartment
to show that she was a judge, just her briefcase by the door.

"You have 'Alice's Adventures in Wonderland,' I see. I was
going to buy that to send to my daughter. Do you think she'd like
it? She's only seven."

"I don't know, I think she may be just a little young. I have
almost all of Lewis Carroll."

"Do you know the tea party scene between the Mad Hatter,
the Dormouse, the March Hare and Alice?" He found the place

and began to read. " 'Then you should say what you mean,' " the March Hare went on. 'I do' Alice hastily replied, 'at least—at least I mean what I say—that's the same thing, you know.'

" 'Not the same thing a bit!' said the Hatter. 'Why, you might just as well say that "I see what I eat" is the same thing as "I eat what I see"!' "

He smiled at her and continued. " 'You might just as well say,' added the Dormouse, which seemed to be talking in his sleep, "I breathe when I sleep" is the same thing as "I sleep when I breathe." ' "

She laughed and gave him an amaretto with ice.

"And of course, Alicia, the trial at the end of the book, with the crazy Queen of Hearts as the judge. Do you remember the Queen of Hearts? She was constantly crying 'Off with their heads!' "

She laughed again and tossed her head back. "Yes, off with their heads! Marvelous. The trial of the Knave of Hearts accused of stealing the Queen's tarts."

He lifted his drink to her. "In India we have a similar fable. I don't know if it was based on Carroll. I doubt it. But we have a fable of a young woman who disappears down a hole into a strange land."

"I would love to see India some day."

"Yes, you must come. I would love to show it to you."

He looked at her curiously and put his drink down and switched off the lamp above his head, and came over to her and took her in his arms and kissed her. It was a long and searching kiss, and finally she moved him away.

"I don't know, Rajiv."

"You don't know what?"

"I think maybe you should go."

"I will go, Alicia, but you must promise to see me Tuesday might. It will be my last night."

He leaned across and kissed her again and held her. She could feel the strength in his arms, and she whispered his name.

He stood away from her at the door and smiled at her.

"You are a very beautiful woman, Alicia. You will have your time in India someday, I know."

She slowly shut the door and looked at herself in the hallway mirror and touched the lines around her eyes. She had almost told him not to kiss her, not to get involved with her because she'd been alone too long and had forgotten how to love someone.

SHE DROVE TO Madison for the two days of the conference and on Tuesday drove back to Milwaukee. Her speech had been poorly received; only a few people spoke to her afterwards. The judges mostly ignored her and went out to dinner with their wives. She took off her convention badge and went to a French film at the University Arts Club by herself. All weekend she felt she was two people: one, the judge, still moving to the rhythms of the office, and the other some detached, faceless woman curiously watching the judge, a woman dressed in a long, white, Victorian dress holding a white umbrella, standing in sunlight, but always faceless.

On Tuesday they walked together down into the Third Ward, and had dinner at an Italian restaurant in an old renovated warehouse building. He laughed at her careful Italian pronunciation when she ordered for them. She felt flushed and excited like a student. She remembered eating at the little trattorias on the edge of the Arno in Florence. She could still hear the sounds of her Italian friends calling good night to each other. "Ciao, Serafina," "Ciao, Giulietta." "Ciao, Alicia." She had always wanted to go back to Florence. Someday she would.

Slowly they walked back to her apartment and stopped at the same bench. She took his hand and again sat watching the boats.

The old white-haired doorman in the lobby of her apartment building said, "Good evening, Judge," to her as he held the door for them. Rajiv was walking behind her and didn't hear him.

In her apartment she had chilled a bottle of wine. He picked up her new Yeats book and looked through it. He began to read her "Down by the Salley Gardens." She watched his mouth as he read in his English accent.

"Down by the salley gardens my love and I did meet;
She passed the salley gardens with little snow-white feet.
She bid me take love easy, as the leaves grow on the tree;
But I, being young and foolish, with her would not agree."

He closed the book and smiled at her. He had a gift for her, wrapped in pink tissue, that he removed from his jacket pocket. It was a silk scarf of flowers, from Bombay. "Here, let me put it on you, Alicia." He draped it over her head in the fashion of an Indian woman. He also had another small piece of blue tissue paper which he opened. There were earrings in the tissue, filigreed silver with dark red stones.

She went to the mirror and put on the earrings. She looked in the mirror and touched her hair and saw the woman in the white dress again, but now her face was visible and she wore the silk flowered scarf around her hair and silver earrings. She was beautiful, a beautiful mysterious woman, as intricate as the circles of filigreed silver in the lovely earrings.

He came to her and put his arms around her and stood behind her at the mirror. She turned to him and led him into her bedroom, and she made love for the first time in several years.

O N WEDNESDAY MORNING he was gone. She drove to the courthouse alone and she was wearing his scarf around her throat and the earrings. She looked at her wristwatch. Minnie Mouse seemed very happy. But Minnie was always happy. She listened to a Mozart tape as she drove. Had her life changed? Did she still have snakes in her hair? There were no snakes. Perseus had slain Medusa by diverting her gaze with the brightness of his shield and then he chopped off her head. So, she wasn't Medusa any more, or even the Queen of Hearts. She knew she was a complicated woman, but she also knew she was a woman who could still love and be loved.

H EAR YE, hear ye, hear ye, the United States Court for the Eastern District of Wisconsin is now in session, the Honorable Alicia Beauchamp, Judge, presiding. Please rise. God save this honorable court and the United States." The clerk rapped her gavel again, Judge Beauchamp sat down in her judge's chair. She was wearing the earrings but she'd left the scarf in her chambers folded in a carved sandalwood box from India that she'd found in Madison.

"United States of America vs. John Gakubiak, 90 C 126."

The clerk handed her the file.

She put on her glasses and smiled briefly at the lawyers and the defendant as they approached the bench. "Good morning, gentlemen," she said. "I am going to deny the government's motion for certification of an interlocutory appeal. There is no compelling question of law involved. If you want to appeal my ruling on the motion *in limine,* Mr. Gibbons, I suggest you do so after the trial, not before. You of course will have that opportunity. In any event, we'll go forward on the 26th."

"Your Honor, may I be heard?" Gibbons said. "After the trial will be too late, Judge. The damage will already have been done if the jury is given the opportunity to consider the exhibits."

"Well, you can object to each one as it's offered, and I'll consider each objection. Anything that should be excluded will be excluded. Likewise Mr. Johnstone can object to each government exhibit as it's offered."

"That's still not acceptable to the government, your Honor. We should have the right to prepare our case in advance of trial, knowing what evidence of the defendant will be excluded *a priori.*"

"What do you mean, *a priori?*"

"I mean ahead of time."

"Why don't you just say what you mean?"

"I apologize. Nevertheless, I object, Your Honor."

"Gentlemen, both sides will be ready for trial on the 26th. I have twelve motions waiting for me on my 10:00 call and twenty cases on my 11:00 set call. Motion of the government denied."

She stood up and the clerk rapped the gavel once.

Judge Beauchamp went back into her chambers and locked her door. She had been away for, what? Four days? Now she was back and nothing had changed. Black is the color of justice. Black will always be the color of justice. She opened her desk and removed the flowered scarf from the sandalwood box. She touched the silk scarf to her face and closed her eyes. The box would become the reliquary of her feelings for Rajiv, but life would not permit her that, and she knew that the texture of his presence was already disappearing and she was alone again.

Investiture

WHEN CHARLES RIORDAN AWOKE this morning he immediately noticed the plastic bag on the dresser in his bedroom. Last night, shopping at Walgreen's, he had suddenly, inexplicably, changed the after-shave he used. Instead of Old Spice, he bought a tiny travel bottle of English Leather. Then he bought a different antiperspirant (Faberge) and talcum powder (Pinaud). When he emerged from the shower this morning and opened the new plastic bottles, he covered himself with entirely different fragrances. The new fragrances would, he hoped, protect him from the harshness of this day.

Today would be a harsh day. An 87-year-old woman client was dying, and she controlled a $5 million estate that she was going to leave in trust to an order of nuns in Chicago. He had prepared her will. He was named as trustee. The sole beneficiary of the trust was the order of nuns. He would meet with the Sister Superior and two priests at St. Joseph's Hospital at noon. If the will was signed, it would provide the order with more than $300,000 a year and an income of $3,000 a month in fees for him as trustee. He had worked to get himself this appointment all his life. Now, at 68, at the end of his career, the income from the trust would be his pension, together with with Social Security and his small savings. It would enable him to retire and leave Chicago for a retirement apartment he had rented in Arizona. His wife died six years ago and their two children now lived at opposite ends of the country.

Today would be one of the most important days of his life, and in order to face it, he would camouflage his usual fear and uncertainty with the cosmetics of powerful men. He would close this. Just this one more deal and he could quit.

It wasn't really a "deal," he told himself. No, of course not. It was a will signing. But it had a peculiar quirk: his client, who had contributed to the order of nuns all her life and had for several years lived as a lay person in the convent with the sisters, insisted, as a condition of her final gift, that she be admitted to the order as a nun. She would then close her eyes and die in peace. Those were her final instructions to him a week ago, and since then she'd grown weaker each day. She was ravaged by cancer and she wanted to die. She'd never told him of these conditions when he'd drawn the will two years ago, but as she was dying, suddenly she wanted to be admitted to the sisterhood. He hadn't said anything about it to the priest or the Sister Superior at the convent. He'd put off opening the subject. He thought he'd talk to them at the hospital today. If she didn't sign the will, though, and exercise her power of appointment, the entire estate would pass under the original trust to collateral relatives and he would not be appointed trustee.

He picked out his white shirt carefully, not a frayed collar today. Most of his shirts had tiny threads fraying at the collars and cuffs. He wore his best suit, a black suit, black would be proper for the priests, and for the nuns, and for the ritual of the will. He was still a good practicing Catholic. He selected a navy blue tie with silver moons and asteroids. He'd shined his shoes carefully the night before. He brushed his hat. It was a gray, soft hat from Marshall Field's, with a small splayed red feather. He looked at himself in the hall mirror; light blue eyes, a thin face, a few red splotches on his cheeks from years of drinking. He'd quit the year before his wife died and joined AA. He had the thin Riordan lips of his father, and the watery, tired, blue eyes of a failed, sad man. But today, in the black suit and gray hat, wearing the secret new lotions, he looked confident. He decided to cut the feather off his hat band. It was too showy and he snipped it off with his manicure scissors.

Charles Riordan lived surrounded by his books on Irish history and literature in a modest, one-bedroom apartment on Grace Street, on the North Side of Chicago. This morning, as he dressed, he carefully brushed dust off his shoulders and then put on his monogrammed, white silk scarf and black overcoat. He did look like he belonged, like a responsible probate lawyer, a counsel that could be trusted, an old friend of the client and the parish. At least he wasn't wearing that foolish red feather in his hat. Lately he noticed some of the lawyers his age were wearing hats downtown that signified their secret longings. Sherlock Holmes caps, captains' yachting caps, even cowboy hats. He wasn't that senescent, not yet; just the solace of the new cosmetics would be enough. He'd wear his real hat in Arizona, the beret of a poet, an artist's beret.

The client, Beatrice Taylor, had been sent to him by an old friend, a parish priest from St. Benedict's on Irving Park. Riordan was introduced to Beatrice Taylor 40 years ago. She was then already a selfish woman, living on a trust fund from her father, and she never married. It was an irrevocable trust administered by a bank as trustee, and she was given income only during her lifetime, with a general power to appoint the principal. She'd become dissatisfied with the bank and hated the trust officers who fought with her over her income. She trusted him and she wanted him to replace the bank as trustee, as her final gesture of contempt for the bank. After his death, her niece, who had received a legacy, would act as trustee. She'd dangled the power of appointment in front of him and the order of nuns all her life, never quite getting around to exercising it. At her direction he'd drawn the will establishing the trust two years ago, but she had always put off signing it, and it had sat in her file. As she grew older, he began to see her face as that of a pouting, dyspeptic, ceramic queen, an ancient, evil queen of angels, her face caked with the patinas of age and selfishness. A week ago, when he last saw her in the hospital, she pursed her dry lips. "How are you Beatrice?" he'd asked, reaching to touch her fingers. "Sister Beatrice Taylor, Charles," she whispered, her eyes glistening behind the tiny spectacles as she gasped for breath. "Sister

Beatrice Taylor, Charles," she whispered, and clung to his wrist with her bony hand. Then she told him about her desire to be admitted to the order as a nun as a condition of her gift.

This morning after his coffee and roll at Wertheim's at Irving and Lincoln he walked slowly to mass at St. Benedict's. He remembered seeing the older Richard Daley coming from mass at St. Peter's on Madison Street, and now, as he touched the holy water to his fingers and face, he wondered about the former mayor. Mayor Daley had nodded to him once. "Hello, Counsel," he'd said. How did Daley know he was a lawyer? Maybe the brief case? Or the frazzled look? Maybe he remembered him from the old neighborhood. He never knew Daley but he also grew up in Bridgeport.

He knelt in one of the pews at St. Benedict's and closed his eyes. Was Daley really flying around in heaven with feathered wings, a florid-faced angel? Were all the dead judges and lawyers from Bridgeport, some of whom he had known as a child, flying around with Daley? What a strange band of angels they all would make. And would he be joining them soon? Would he soon be flying with them? Wasn't some angel with huge feathered wings waiting for him? He thought of the mosaic of the two Greek mythological flyers at the 120 North LaSalle Street Building across from the County Building, the mosaic of two Greek men in white shorts, flying on huge feathered wings. They looked like lawyers who'd lost their clothes and wallets in the Daley Center. Who were they? He knew they were supposed to be Icarus and Daedalus, Daedalus the father and Icarus the son. Icarus flew so close to the sun that the wax on his wings melted. That had happened to a lot of lawyers in this town.

He opened his eyes and stared at the faces of the ceramic angels surrounding the altar. One of them did look like his client, a fat-faced ancient queen cupid, a selfish pout, lips puckered and eyes vacant. Sister Beatrice. He tried to shake all this out of his head, He didn't want this kind of confusion, the hierarchy of floating angels waiting for him. He wanted certainty, the arms of Christ around him, and repose. He was afraid and uncertain of death. He closed his eyes and said a prayer and calmed down.

He took the El down to his office on Monroe Street. He rented a small office in a six-office suite. The receptionist, a woman in her 20's, Theresa, waved to him as he walked in, and then she shook her head. There were no messages. She was talking on the phone to one of her friends. "I was like so bored, I go 'I want to dance. I want to like do something, not just sit here,' and he goes 'Drink your beer.' So I go 'Shut up,' and he like freaks out and throws his beer at me. It missed me. Like just a little on my hair. I was so pissed." He closed his door. Her voice became just a murmur. He wished he could invent a machine, a CAT Scanner, where people could stick their heads in and with one jolt, "go" and "like" would permanently be removed from their vocabulary. Half the country's work force under 30 would suddenly become mute. Theresa was nice to him, though. She put his mail aside for him every day and was always cheerful — with her spiked hair and bright clothes. She was really the only cheerful person in the office.

There were five lawyers in the suite, all men, and three of them had a small insurance defense firm. One younger man helped them answer their court call in a space-for-services arrangement. Riordan had the fifth office and one office was vacant. CHARLES J. RIORDAN was lettered on the frosted window of the heavy, old-fashioned, varnished door. The men in the suite weren't friends, but they all got along and his rent was low, $350. He did his own typing behind the closed door. He didn't have a word processor, but he had an old IBM Electric and hunted and pecked on envelopes and a few letters. The word processing service on the fifth floor did his wills. That's what his practice had dwindled down to now, almost all small probate matters. He was good at drafting wills, and the complicated trust he'd drawn for Beatrice Taylor pleased him because of its good draftsmanship. He'd worked very hard on it and had taken it to a friend who specialized in estate planning, who polished it for him. He liked drafting wills and contracts. He used to be able to try injury cases before a jury, but he no longer wanted to go to court and gradually the cases had disappeared. The good injury cases were chased and anyway, he didn't have the stomach at 68 for trial work. He liked probate. It was clean work and the fees were enough so that he could still net $25,000 a year after taxes, even with his dwindling practice. At least he hadn't been indicted. How many lawyers and judges had been convicted in the Greylord investigations? Sixty-nine? Seventy? Almost the same number as his age. Had he ever bribed a judge? No. That was his one major accomplishment—a lawyer for 45 years and he'd never bribed a judge. Maybe he would get a plaque from the Bar Association.

When he left his office he locked his telephone. It had a device that locked it from being used, and he always locked it. Then he locked his office door. He walked out on Clark Street and suddenly he thought of Leopold Bloom, Joyce's character in "Ulysses." Why Bloom? Because he'd been thinking of the two Greek flyers, because he, Riordan, was really ineffectual like the two flyers, like Bloom, even this morning, covered with the secret cosmetics, but he couldn't be ineffectual, not today. He had to perform just this one day, dear God.

As he walked to the bus stop he continued thinking of Bloom and Joyce. Joyce had met his wife, Nora, at Finn's Hotel in Dublin. The worn name of Finn's Hotel was still slightly visible on the wall of Trinity College. He'd seen photos of it. The hotel was built into the wall. Nora worked there as a chambermaid in 1904 when Joyce met her. If he'd close this trust (it wasn't a deal), he would go to Dublin to see the walls of Trinity and sit in St. Stephen's Green and wander the book stalls along the banks of the Liffey. He'd go to the Abbey Theatre. He had promised himself Dublin, first Dublin and then Arizona. Joyce had created Stephen Dedalus. Was he named after the Greek Daedalus? Of course he was. He nodded his head unconsciously and smiled as he showed his senior's pass to the conductor. He would catch the 157 bus on Washington to Michigan, and the 151 to Diversey to the hospital.

He sat down heavily and stared out at the Picasso on the Daley

Center Plaza. At Michigan Avenue he waited for a northbound bus. It was cold early in November, and he was chilled. He could hear the sound of his own heart beating in the chambers of his ears, even over the sound of traffic. That had been happening to him lately, the sound of his own heart swelling in the chambers of his ears.

The bus came and he found a seat beside an older woman, being careful not to touch or brush her as he sat down. If he wasn't thinking about death, he thought about money. He thought of the two envelopes he'd gotten earlier this week enclosing checks, one check for a real estate closing for $500, and the other for a will and powers of attorney, $350. He summoned up the two envelopes containing the checks. One envelope had a stamp with a heart inscription, the other a blue stamp with a gold medallion honoring our dead in the Iraq war. The two return-address labels also bore red hearts. He remembered the pastel color of each check, a desert scene on one check. What was on the other? A ship, an eagle adrift in a canyon? The mnemonics of counting his money soothed him. His fees this month were only $1,000. It was an awful month. Last month was $2,200, next month would perhaps be over $4,000. Again, "if." "If" he could close a small estate, "if" he could get it approved by the bullying judge. It was always "if," but this counting of fees due him usually brought him some repose, but they were dwindling. Every month the total was smaller.

As they moved out over the Michigan Avenue bridge past the shops of Michigan Avenue, he closed his eyes and catalogued his savings accounts. Bell Federal ($5,000); Talman ($7,000); Citicorp ($8,000); First Chicago (5,000). Twenty-five thousand dollars. Some lawyers had millions stashed away. The dark suited, gaunt-faced corporate lawyers on LaSalle Street heading for their suburban trains, groups of partners, walking together in deferential order. Some of them had more than a million stashed in a secret place. What did he have in his secret place? A box at Lincoln Federal with his wife's rings, a photograph of his mother and father, his army discharge certificate, a swimming medal from high school, a lock of both children's hair. Thinking of money didn't calm him this morning, it only upset him. The pinstriped lawyers of Kenilworth and Winnetka with their calfskin brief cases ... they were like sepulchral figures mocking him. He wouldn't let them upset him this morning. Who was the angel waiting for him? Was it his wife? Was she in the secret place waiting with her dark wings folded, her hand reaching out to him? Could she help him anoint Sister Beatrice?

They passed the Water Tower and he saw a *Tribune* on the seat across from him, and opened it to read.

When he arrived at St. Joseph's he walked into the lobby and then into the gift shop, where he was waited on by a young nun. She wore a light blue habit and a white plastic name badge. Sister Regina.

"How may I help you, sir?"

"I want to buy a card for someone who's very ill."

"I'll show you some cards."

The young nun had high-colored cheeks, and natural beauty, the natural beauty of her innocence and clarity.

He looked down and saw a pile of tiny silver religious medals. "I don't think I want a card. I'll take one of these medals. How much are they?"

"One dollar, sir. Our Lady of Czestochowa."

He opened his wallet and handed her a dollar, and she dropped the medal into a small plastic bag with some brochures advertising the shop's products. He looked at her clear eyes, and he seemed to be looking down a blue tunnel into her repose. As she handed him the bag, their hands touched.

"Excuse me," he said.

"God bless you, sir," she answered, smiling at him.

"Thank you, Sister. God bless you, too."

He took the elevator to the seventh floor. He got off and went over to the nurses' station and asked for Beatrice Taylor. One of the supervising nurses at the station turned to him.

"I don't think Beatrice is going to last the afternoon. If you want to see her, you'd better go in now." She was a tough, direct woman and she was pulling charts. "I'm going there now. You can come with me. Are you a family member?"

"No, I'm her lawyer."

"Do you have papers for her to sign? Do you need witnesses?" She held a stack of clipboards in her hands.

"I have a will for her to sign, if she's still able to sign."

"As far as I'm concerned, counselor, they're all able to sign."

He hesitated and turned to the younger nurse at the desk. "Have there been two priests and a nun here to see Beatrice Taylor?"

"No," she answered, "no one's asked for her."

The senior nurse had gone down the hall. He followed her. He never liked hospitals, the sterile odors, the hiss of oxygen, and the smell of death, brief glimpses of patients in the rooms, mouths agape. The nurse had called him "counsel," just like Mayor Daley.

She pointed to a room and preceded him inside. He could see that Beatrice had grown much weaker. She didn't open her eyes as the nurse leaned over the bed. There was a bottle of fluid dripping into her wrist through a tube and another tube out from the bed to a bottle filling with her urine. There was no light in the room. The nurse turned a lamp on over her face, and he saw how mottled and bruised her skin seemed, all color drained from it.

"Beatrice," the nurse bent over and called to her in her ear. "Beatrice, wake up, wake up, Beatrice." There was no reaction. "Beatrice, there's someone here to see you."

Her eyes fluttered for a moment, and the nurse touched her temples with water from a glass at the bedside.

"Beatrice, your lawyer is here. What's your name, counsel?"

"Riordan. Charles Riordan." He could feel his heart starting to flutter in his ears.

"Beatrice, Mr. Riordan is here to see you. I'm going to sit you up. Get up, Beatrice."

"Sleep."

"No, you're not sleeping. Get up. You're not asleep." she

propped pillows behind her and gently pulled her up. "You have to sign some papers, Beatrice. She's up now, counsel. Keep talking to her. I'll get another witness."

"Can she sign?"

"She can if you sign for her. They do it all the time."

The nurse snapped her fingers in front of Beatrice's face three times quickly and then nodded to him and left the room. He leaned over to her and for a moment he felt a great wave of solicitude for her.

"Beatrice, it's Charles Riordan. Do you understand me?"

The eyes stared at him.

"Do you know me, Beatrice? Can you sign your name? I have your will."

He took the tiny silver medal the nun had given him and put it in her left hand and closed her hand around it. "Can you sign this, Beatrice?"

"Charles?"

"Yes, it's me."

"I'm so tired."

"Will you sign this will?" He put the pen in her right hand and guided her fingers into a signature. The touch of her hand was like the touch of death and in this final ceremony he might be accused of fraud. He knew that, but it had to be done, this investiture. He had to do it for her and for himself.

The nurses came back into the room. "Did she sign it?"

"Yes."

"Go back to sleep now, Beatrice." The nurse turned the light off. "Go to sleep." She put her down gently.

The two women in the starched uniforms witnessed the will and handed it back to him.

"Thank you," he told them. He then turned back to the bed and touched Beatrice Taylor's forehead and hair with his fingers. Had he really set her free? Had he hinged her with feathered wings to fly to the sun? If so, she had also set him free. He would never have to go back to the eviction courts or to the divorce courts or close neighborhood real estate deals to make a living. He would have his trustee's fees for the rest of his life.

When he returned to the waiting room he asked again if the parish priests and the Sister Superior from the convent had come. They hadn't, and he decided not to wait for them. He would phone them and tell them she'd signed the will.

When he left the hospital the outside air hit his face, but as he walked away to the bus he still sensed the touch of her skin and her dry hair on his fingertips, and the odor of her death was in his nostrils.

Solo

H E HAD REFUSED to accede. So they fired him.

He had refused to accede to the firm policy of 2,000 annual billable hours. It was an absolute. He knew about it but had defied it. He'd turned in only 1,750 hours again, but it wasn't enough this year, and he had refused to pad his time. His senior associate had told him just to go back to his office, review his time sheets, and come back with the missing 250 hours. He refused to do it. So they let him go, graciously, but nevertheless absolutely, with two months severance ($12,000), one month for each year, and the proffered services of an outplacement service which he had also refused. Instead he took the $12,000, told them he was going solo, and leased an office.

The office was in a northern suburb of Chicago in a new shopping center done in the style of a French manor house. He bought an antique mahogany desk with an embossed hand-tooled, gold-bordered leather writing surface ($1,500), and three sets of antique lawyers bookcases with glass doors ($1,000). Into these he inserted a new set of Illinois Annotated Statutes ($1,500). The salesman had also tried to sell him the United States Code Annotated at a discount price on installments, and he thought about it, but he had other plans. He bought a good computer and a printer ($2,500), and installed a phone with a nine-number memory, redial, call waiting, and call forwarding ($750). He had an instinctive fondness for hand-held plastic. Just the touch of new things seemed to assuage him, and bring him to a tactile sense of impending wealth and power. He thought of buying a FAX machine, but they wanted $500.

There was also the matter of the security deposit, the first month's rent ($750) on a year's lease with an option for another year. He bought an adding machine, a small, quick gray plastic machine with blue glowing numerals that showed the sums on a tiny slit. A postal meter ($150 deposit). An answering machine ($100). He practiced his message several times until it sounded right. He didn't want to sound anxious. He wanted a confident, strong voice on the tape.

What else? He bought a throw rug, an Icelandic heraldic design. What are Icelandic heralds, he'd asked the blonde saleswoman as she showed him the rug. She looked up at him and seemed really puzzled by the question, so he stopped interrogating her and bought the rug. She was just trying to make her living in a world of tangled skeins, he knew that. She'd showed him another rug she thought had been woven from albino yaks or was it white Llamas? He'd meant to ask her but instead paid $950 in cash and walked out with the Icelandic rug twisted into a tight roll under his arm. Now he was his own herald. She did remind him of Andrea though, the same cool blonde fragility.

He'd spent almost $10,000 and he still needed a sign for the door and malpractice insurance. So he did the sign ($150) but delayed on the malpractice insurance. Then he bought a cheap fare to London ($350 round trip) and sat in the rose gardens of Bloomsbury and tried to sort things through.

He watched a couple sitting on a bench in front of the statue of Ghandi in the rose garden. She was sitting on his lap, and they were kissing. After a moment she got up and walked over to Ghandi seated like a Buddha and touched his toe, then went back to her lover's lap, put her arms around him and kissed him again. Everyone in London seemed to be kissing—couples on the Tube, couples on the street, couples in the gardens—and he was alone. The previous evening he'd gone in a taxi to seen Anthony Hopkins in *M. Butterfly.* Hopkins played the part of a French diplomat who had fallen in love with a Chinese opera star in Peking and had an affair with her for twenty years. She turned out not only to have been a spy but a man. How could Hopkins possibly not have known she was a man? Or had he known? In the end, Hopkins made himself up into Madame Butterfly, smearing on the white makeup of a Kabuki, painting on her red eyebrows, putting on her silken robe and a high, coiled, black wig, and then with his back to the audience, he held up a dagger glittering in the spotlight and plunged the dagger into his stomach.

The white silk and blood, the yellow and blue streamers, the silk curtains covered with green dragons, the wailing sounds of the Kabuki violin and flute—it was very beautiful, very intricate and sad. Andrea came swirling into his mind again as he listened to the applause. The last time he saw her was at the office. She was wearing the same kind of white silk blouse the blonde saleswoman had worn.

He and Andrea had made love twice. Once in Asheville, North Carolina, at a Holiday Inn where they'd been sent out as a deposition team on a tax case. Once in Rockford at another Holiday Inn when they'd rented a car and driven to a firm-sponsored video presentation on employment termination claims. That last time had been a month ago. On the night he'd been fired, he'd knocked on her office door to tell her, and she'd been strangely radiant so he didn't say anything. She closed the door and kissed him. She was rushing to meet her parents and leaving for Japan tomorrow on vacation. He'd forgotten about her trip to Japan. She was meeting a law school friend in Kobe, and they were going inn-trekking. So he left without telling her and kissed her goodbye and wished her a good trip. She said she just wanted a rest from the telephone and the demands of the partners. She just couldn't take it anymore. She laughed and said that maybe she and Nancy would both find jobs teaching English in Japan. Two weeks later he received a netsuke doll with a tiny scroll with a single red brush stroke. He showed it to a Japanese waitress he knew, and she told him the letter was the Japanese word for "friend".

So instead of waiting for her, he went to London.

On the way back to the hotel from *M. Butterfly,* walking the deserted streets in Holburn, he thought about the character's suicide. He could do that for the firm. If he was willing to do that for the firm and admit that he'd been mistaken, they might ask him back. But in his fantasy he would just pretend to kill himself. He would get a collapsing spring fake dagger and a pill of fake blood. He'd seen them in a magic shop near the hotel. The English loved magic. The shop had hand buzzers, snakes, spiders, masks, invisible ink, whoopee cushions, blood capsules, plastic vomit, and two daggers, one rubber and then the one he wanted, spring action, collapsible. He would sneak into his old office in full Kabuki garb and makeup about 7:00 some evening while the summer associates were being herded to an expensive French restaurant by some of the partners and their wives. The wives had come into the city to make a tour of the new firm library. One woman would turn and see him through the glass panels, seated at his desk under a single light, in his robe and wig. He would cut his tongue for her, making himself into a Kabuki right in front of her. He would hold the glittering knife up high and all would turn to watch him, even the summer associates in their new pin-striped suits and fresh silk print dresses. He would slowly bow to them, spread the arms of his robe and shove the collapsible knife into his gut, slowly dropping his head onto the desk with the capsule of blood spewing from the corner of his mouth. There would be screams and then when they were sufficiently terrified, he'd just get up and leave. It might be a little dramatic, perhaps bizarre, but it would have been a perfect exit.

The first day he moved into his new office he'd learned that he'd made the mistake of renting across the hall from a dental suite. The odors of clove and wintergreen came wafting through the air shaft and by midafternoon he felt queasy. Also, the walls were too thin, almost without insulation, and he could hear the insurance agent next door wheedling his clients for premiums in a brash, arrogant voice that apparently paid for the white Eldorado parked in his parking space. At noon he watched the man gun his car away. Always people gunning their cars away in this suburb, tires screeching while they're talking on car phones. Later that week, he passed his card out to a group of real estate women. He hoped he might get some closings. One of them brashly told him she'd send him closings if he'd split fees with her. The going rate for a house closing was $350. She wanted a referral fee of $175 and she would guarantee two closings a week. If they worked well together, the two closings a week could easily become three or even four. He quickly calculated it would give him almost $1,400 a month as a base. When he said no, she smiled and patted his hand. She gave him her card.

He went to a few meetings of the Chamber of Commerce, the Lions Club, the Kiwanis. Everyone was friendly, and he handed out more cards. He even ate roasted bear meat at the Kiwanis picnic, the annual men's cookout. He mailed announcements of the opening of his office to his suburban high school and college friends. Many of them had returned to the suburbs as young marrieds. He received a few polite congratulatory notes.

When Andrea returned from Japan she called him. She'd of course heard that he'd been let go and had received his card from London. She said she was shocked. She was swamped with work, working Saturdays and Sundays. She promised they'd be together in two weeks. She wanted to drive out and see his office. She missed him very much and wanted to make love again. Two days later she sent him a plant.

He got his first case and he needed it badly because he was almost out of money. He had savings of $5,000, in addition to the severance check, but last month took over half his savings. The first fee was a $1,500 retainer from a sullen, acne-faced teenager. His mother hired him to defend her son against a DUI charge. He didn't know what he was doing, but the assistant states attorney was kind to him, and because the client had no record, struck the

DUI charge for a plea to reckless driving. The client was fined $500 and sent to six weeks of driver education with a six month suspension of license. The $1,500 fee paid the rent, the phone, and part of his initial printing bill, and left him $100.

Two elderly sisters called for wills. When quoted $350 each, the woman on the phone hesitated and said that she'd call back. He knew they were shopping lawyers. Later, the woman called and asked him, if she'd keep it simple, would he do a will for $250? He agreed. She paid his bill without complaint, and then the second sister called and ordered her will. So he had planted three seeds, a scrofulous teenager and two elderly women with lists of porcelain cups. Still, it was the beginning of his client garden, and that's how he thought of it, each client a tiny growing seed. If he took care of them, he would survive.

Andrea drove out to see him in a new red Honda Accord. He asked her to spend the night at his apartment. Instead, she insisted on treating them to rooms at a Marriott that resembled a Japanese tea house, a small cluster of houses around a garden. They made love until he finally collapsed over her, exhausted. In the morning, when they said goodbye, she offered to lend him a thousand dollars, but he refused. She had to work that Sunday night and then fly to Cleveland in the morning.

"Don't give up, Mark," she said. "It's easy just to give up and start looking for another job. You're doing fine. Just remember that you're your own boss. No one tells you to fly to Cleveland tomorrow."

"It's a nice car."

"I like it, but it's just a car. It doesn't put its arms around me. It doesn't want to make love to me."

"Have a good trip."

"You know, if you keep going, Mark, maybe I could quit too. We could become partners."

"Is that a proposal?"

"No, that's a proposition." She flashed her smile and he stood and watched her drive away and gave her a thumbs-up sign.

The next week he turned to plastic for the first time for a cash advance. He had a three thousand-dollar credit limit with Citibank Visa and he drew down half of it, paid his student loan, his office rent, and his apartment rent, and let the office phone slide. He called on the states attorney's office, inquiring whether he could get a part-time appointment trying cases in a suburban court. The man smiled at him. You have to get in line, he told him. There are 2,000 lawyers in the county, half of them under 35, and there are at least 150 on a waiting list for assistantships or public defenders jobs. First thing, get on the list, but join the local Republican party and donate a thousand dollars to the Central Committee. The donation is no guarantee of a job, but it puts you on the list, and there's a fairly high turnover rate, maybe six months to a year.

He didn't have six months to a year. He went to some of the local banks and passed his card out to the trust officers. They greeted him with the small-town camaraderie of long established local bankers. They'd be pleased to serve his clients. They didn't get many walk-ins though, looking for lawyers. Most of the local people had their own lawyers and had been with them for years. One man gave him a calendar. Another a leather-covered kit of will forms naming his bank as executor and trustee.

Then he got two real estate deals, both from having networked the local offices. No one asked him for a referral fee. They were both residential closings. One was for a family in California whose mother had died. They mailed him a $1,000 retainer to probate the mother's will in Illinois and handle the sale of her home. It was a simple probate. It would take six months, and he was to hold the buyer's $25,000 earnest money deposited in a trust account. He went to the trust officer who'd given him the will kit and opened the trust account and deposited the $25,000. The man shook his hand and thanked him. The trust officer told him that in exchange for the deposit they'd stop the monthly service charge on his checking account and provide him with free checks. It was the least they could do. He didn't say anything. He'd give the bank a week. If they didn't reciprocate and send him some business, he'd move the account. They had collection work, foreclosures, guardianships, wills. They could send him business. He was learning. You couldn't just sit back and let them walk over you.

Still, he couldn't make it through the month on the $1,000 retainer and the other closing, so he drew his last $1,500 from his Visa and applied for two more cards, from two other banks. He knew that he was weaving a web, a dangerous web, and he might not be able to break out of it.

Basketball was still fun for him, and jogging. He shot baskets after work. Every night he tried to jog three miles around the park, out to the reservoir and back to his office. One night after jogging, he was in the office, and a woman called about a divorce. Her husband was always working. She was left alone with two young children. She thought he was having a love affair. He could hear ice clinking and a child crying. What did he charge for a divorce? She had little money of her own. Could he force the husband to pay her fee? Could she put him out of the house and still get maintenance and child support? She had to have at least $1,500 a month to live.

Would she pay a small retainer fee, he asked? No, she suddenly began shrieking, I can't pay a retainer fee. All you lawyers are the same. All of you only want money from me. I have no money. Can't you understand that? She began sobbing. "Madame, have you tried Legal Aid?" He gave her the number and gently hung up. The phone rang again, but he didn't answer it. She called several more times, but he still didn't answer.

Only one of the new credit cards came, and he immediately drew the $3,000 limit and paid his bills. It had happened so quickly. He was into the banks for $6,000 at 20 percent interest and he'd only been practicing on his own for two months. He knew now that he'd spent his severance check foolishly. He didn't need that expensive furniture or the trip to London. He wished he could start over again. He should have budgeted each month and been extremely careful with the money.

Andrea was in New York working on a case. He hadn't seen her in three weeks. She called him one night at his apartment while he was making dinner.

"Why don't you fly here and meet me this weekend, Mark?"

"I can't afford it."

"I'll pay for the ticket."

"No. I can't keep letting you pay for me."

She was silent. He could hear ice clinking in a glass, the same sound of the woman calling for a divorce.

"I'm sorry," she said.

"Don't be sorry. There's nothing to be sorry about. It's my problem."

"I keep trying to mother you."

"I could use a mother."

"So how's it going, Mark? How's it really going?"

"It's going okay."

"You don't sound okay. Just get on the plane. Please."

"No."

"Okay. Goodnight, Mark. Why don't you call me sometime? Why am I always calling you?"

She hung up.

That week he got the dog case. A group of neighbors had formed to protest the constant barking of a dog kept in a pen in a house just beyond their cul-de-sac. The dog, he was told, looked like a huge wolf with yellow eyes and a curved tail, and barked incessantly, day and night. It had made the neighborhood insufferable. The group of neighbors had written a polite note to the dog's owners, a young couple. There was no answer. They'd tried a second note and called the local police, but the police refused to intervene. So he was called and met with them over coffee and cookies at one of their houses, and quoted $5,000 as his retainer for an injunction suit.

One of the women challenged him.

"Why $5,000? Isn't that a lot of money for a dog case?"

"No, it isn't. There are a lot of variables to consider."

"What do you mean, variables?" She was like an angry little
bird pecking at him.

"Well, first of all, there's the dog."

"The dog is a given."

He could feel them all staring at him.

"Of course. But not the dog's owners. The couple. They'll
retain their own counsel."

One man nodded at him.

"We'll have to go to court in equity. An injunction is an extra-
ordinary remedy. It's very hard to get. We'll have to show irrepara-
ble damage, lack of an adequate remedy at law." He began to spew
legal jargon.

"Well, do you guarantee this? Do you guarantee we win?" The
woman whipped her glasses off and pointed them at him.

"There's no guarantee. Lawyers aren't allowed to guarantee."

"Why don't we just bribe the judge?" a man said brightly.
"Judges are always being bribed in Cook County. Why don't we
just become Greylords and give the judge the five thousand?"

Everyone laughed but they agreed to the retainer, although the
angry woman said she'd forgotten her checkbook. He told them
he'd pick up the check when he had their complaint ready.

As he left the driveway, the hostess took him to the back of her
yard and he could see the dog through the neighbor's bushes in a
pen under a spotlight. The dog saw them coming and began
growling and barking. It was a beast, a snarling beast of a dog, like
a huge wolf. He could still hear it barking a block away when he
went to his car. No wonder they wanted to shut it up.

That night he tried to call Andrea in New York, but she wasn't
at her hotel, and he didn't leave a message.

Three days later he returned to the client's home for her to
sign the complaint. He'd framed a good complaint, nicely written
on his word processor. He'd driven into Chicago to use the form
books at the library. Then he hired a stenographer at his office
building to transcribe his word processing so it would look profes-
sional. He walked over to the circuit court clerk's office and picked

up the injunction forms. He prepared a summons, a notice of motion, and a draft order. He had sent the dog's owners a letter. If they didn't agree to muzzle the dog or keep it inside permanently, he'd file the lawsuit.

"Oh, Mark," his client said when she came to the door. 'Oh, Mark, I don't know what to say to you. I have your check here but something awful has happened."

"What's happened?"

"They had their dog operated on. They had its vocal cords cut so it can't bark anymore."

He could feel gray wisps drifting into his eyes. He wouldn't show her any sign.

"So you don't need my services?"

She touched his hand. "No. Now we don't need you. The barking has stopped. They must have gotten your letter."

"And had the dog's throat cut?"

"Yes."

She showed him the check made out to him for $5,000 and then asked him to follow her out to the dog's pen. "Can't we pay you something for the letter? I've been authorized to give you $250. They want you to have it."

"No. I don't want anything."

The dog was immediately alert to their coming. It jumped up and down, clawing against the chain link fence, working its jaws furiously—but it was silent. She was right; they had slit its vocal chords. He stared at the yellow eyes, the vacant almond eyes filled with rage, and he knew the dog had reason to hate him. It was a dog now with the slit chords of a Kabuki, a gray-faced silent dog.

He drove back to his office and shut the blinds. He tried not to think about what had happened and called Andrea again, but she still didn't answer. He had needed that $5,000 desperately. He was so broke. He had $25,000 in the trust fund account. It would be easy to write a check against it. It would just be a loan. He'd pay it back as his luck changed. No one would know. And his luck would change. He looked at his hands. He thought of Hopkin's hands, the gray-chalked Kabuki face, the glittering knife, and then the dog's face, its jaws working to sound its severed chords. No, he wouldn't do it. He would never do it. Somewhere in the dog's yellow eyes and its ultimate silence he had learned something. Things would work themselves out. He was young. Time was on his side. But he was learning that he would have to give and receive injury.

The Ice Horse

S HE SAT IN THE DARK behind the soundproofed glass walls of
the library with a stopwatch in her hand. As each runner
passed the window, her job was to clock his time and enter it
in a computer. It had started as a joke, the late-night running
around the circumference of the office, three laps a mile, but now
it had become a ritual, a very serious ritual, and Cecelia's job was
to handle the stopwatch and punch in the times. At the end of the
workout she'd feed the disc with the times into the word processor
and then stat six copies, one for each man.

As she sat on a table with her legs tucked up underneath her,
the orange light of the computer screen cast the only light in the
room and it highlighted her features. Cecelia Maria Sandoval was a
law student who worked nights as a law clerk and whose dark features and long shining black hair gave her the face of an Aztec
princess. She'd only had the job for a month. She was a first-year
student in a night law school in Chicago and she worked for the
firm for two nights a week, rushing over after her 6:00 contracts
class. At first, they'd given her reams of computer printouts of telephone logs on an antitrust case to scan for spelling errors. Then
they handed her the watch and taught her to use one of the
library's computers, and suddenly she was the night timekeeper for
their track team.

She seldom spoke to any of the runners, and they didn't speak
to her. She was very precise and careful with the times. As the faces

passed by the library, she sat silently in the dark and watched them with a mixture of awe and hatred that she'd reserved for them all her life.

She was assigned as a clerk to the oldest runner, Edward Parkhurst. He was the firm's chief antitrust litigator. He also coached the track team and ran with it. He was a lean-faced, thin-bodied man, about fifty, married with a home in Lake Forest and two daughters in Eastern schools. Edward Parkhurst had been captain of his Dartmouth track team, and on his office wall there was a photograph of him shyly holding a trophy after the meet with Yale in his senior year. There were also two new gold plaques from the last two years. His team had won the plaques for the firm in competition with the other major Chicago law firms.

She soon realized she was more like a night servant to Parkhurst than a legal assistant. She kept his Florentine leather boxes freshly loaded with paper clips, one for large clips, one for small. She supplied him with fresh boxes of tissues, watered his plants, sharpened his pencils, and did the extra personal correspondence filing his secretary left for her. She also carefully stacked the printouts of the runners' times on his bookcase so they would be available to him every morning.

After several weeks some of the members of the track team occasionally began to speak to her. Her relationship with Parkhurst hadn't really changed, except instead of telephone logs he'd given her a few citations to check on interoffice memos. "Harmless stuff, Cecelia," he'd said to her. "You can't hurt us with these. Just follow the uniform system of citation you use at law school. You know, the blue booklet." His hand lingered on hers as he handed her the notes. It was the second time he did that to her. Two days ago, when he'd asked her to carry some books for him down to the library, as he handed her the pile of books his face came close to hers, so close her hair inadvertently touched his cheek. She didn't think about it again. The citations were easy, and before the nightly run she returned them to him. His eyes caught hers for a second, but there was no other signal from him.

The next day was a religious holiday, the Day of the Dead, *el Dia de los Muertes,* and there was a mass at the old church of Our Lady of Guadalupe in her neighborhood on Loomis Street. After the mass all the parishioners walked to the park in a procession in honor of the dead. She held a white lighted candle in her hand and walked behind the priest swinging his censer of incense before her.

When she came to the office that night she still had the smell of incense in her hair and she had kept the stub of the candle in her purse. Instead of immediately switching on the computer in the library, she lit the candle stub and sat with it in the darkness. It was soothing to her, and she was alone. For a moment she closed her eyes and saw herself as a child on a horse in between her grandparents on their tiny ranch in the mountains of New Mexico. It was the only photograph she had of her grandparents—who were now dead—and she treasured it.

"Cecelia, do you like to work by candlelight?" The door had opened, and Edward Parkhurst stood there in his jogging suit.

"Oh, I'm sorry, sir."

He snapped the light on.

"Cecelia, do you look like your mother?"

"My mother?"

He reached out and touched her face with the back of his hand. His hand on her face reminded her of an ugly snake, coiled and ready to strike. Should she stand up?

"I don't understand you, Cecelia," he said to her. He turned away and walked out, snapping off the light and leaving her again in darkness.

A week later he brought a hammer, flashlight, and several rolls of orange luminous tape to her. Instead of the usual workout this night, the men were to run on the street, up Michigan Avenue, over the bridge to the Water Tower, and back to the Art Institute. She was to wait for them with the flashlight and stopwatch in front of the Art Institute lions and clock the runners as they returned. Before they all took the elevator down to the street, he asked her to wrap each runner around the waist with a strand of orange luminous tape. He watched her strangely as she did it, almost as if the wrapping of the men was a ceremony. He said he would carry the hammer to ward off any cars that might aim at him. Cars had been coming too close.

The runners took off up Michigan Avenue but one of them, Jeremy Barthold, stayed with her on the steps. He had twisted an ankle and couldn't run. He invited her across the street for coffee. He was a rather nice man, she thought, and unlike the others, quite friendly. In the restaurant he ordered coffee for each of them.

"Tell me about Mr. Parkhurst," she asked Jeremy.

"What do you mean?"

"All this running. I don't understand it."

"He just likes to compete."

She thought about asking Jeremy some other questions, but she didn't.

"He likes to win. Last week he brought in a fifty-million-dollar jury verdict in an antitrust case. With treble damages, that's a hundred and fifty million. Do you know what the fees are on that?"

"No." She put the stopwatch down between them and glanced at it. The runners had been gone almost ten minutes.

"Try twenty million dollars." He smoothed his blond hair back over his forehead and put on a pair of dark glasses. "My eyes are sensitive to this kind of fluorescent light. They won't be back for at least another fifteen minutes."

She turned the stopwatch toward herself.

"Cecelia, how do you like your job?"

"It's hard with three jobs. I work as a waitress in the afternoon in a restaurant on LaSalle Street, and in the mornings at a legal clinic in the church in our neighborhood. I love that job. But here, Parkhurst hardly gives me hardly anything legal to do, except work with the track team, and I shuffle a few papers."

"It will get better."

"I don't know."

"No, if you'll just be patient, he'll give you more responsibility. They need you, you know."

"They need me?" She laughed, and her white teeth flashed at him.

"Sure. They must have some minority people if they want to work for the city or the government. They need a census that shows at least one Latino, and you're it."

"I don't think so," she said. "They could fire me tomorrow."

He smiled and glanced at the watch and left some money. "Okay, let's go back and time them in."

She stood beside Jeremy on the steps of the Art Institute, watching the snow drift slowly across Michigan Avenue. The first runner came in, stretching his arms at an imaginary tape, and Jeremy caught him and held him. "Way to go Steve!" They were both laughing, and Stephen walked down the sidewalk panting, with his hands on his hips. Jeremy gave him a thumbs-up sign. The second runner came in now, gracefully extending his chest to the imaginary line and Cecelia clocked him and Jeremy slapped his hand in a high-five and the second runner disappeared down the sidewalk into the darkness.

Cecelia stood watching them. *Que diferencia.* These young, white men. They reminded her of white deer running in the darkness, very graceful, very elusive. She and her grandfather would sit for hours in the pine forest in the Sangre de Cristo mountains, absolutely silent, as mute as the ancient stones of the mountains, waiting for the white deer to come to the pool at night to drink in the moonlight. Her grandfather would stretch a piece of rope across a narrowing in the path, fastening it to the two young trees, saplings that would bend with the impact of a deer and catch its throat, not killing it, just stunning it. Then he and Cecelia would creep along the rocks to the animal, its heart beating wildly, legs thrashing, its eyes wild with terror, and her grandfather, with one clean silent drive of the knife, would plunge his knife into the animal's heart. They would carry it home to the grandparents' ranchero, and there would be food for all of them. *Que diferencia.* The lights flashing on the faces of these strange young men. Now came Jonathan and just behind him, Parkhurst, and then very quickly Tom and Peter, all laughing and slapping each other on the backsides. Parkhurst was as happy as she'd ever seen him. He ignored her until finally he came over to her and handed her the hammer. "We're going out for a drink. Please take this back to the office and print out the times." He reached out and took some snowflakes from her hair. He looked at her for a moment and trotted away.

She returned to the office and entered the times into the computer. She fed the disc into the word processor and took the sheets to Parkhurst's office. There was no one in the corridor, only a few young associates in the library working on a brief that had to be at the printers by midnight. They'd been working all Saturday and Sunday on it. One man nodded at her through the window. Another was asleep with his head on his arms.

She put the sheets on the bookcase behind the desk. He had a collection of modern art and groups of photographs. She looked at the faces in the photographs. A young Edward Parkhurst, a law school graduate standing between two older people, a man and a woman she presumed were his parents. It was his version of the photograph of herself on the horse between her grandparents, only instead of short people with dark, weather-worn faces, these people were tall and lean. His father was wearing a suit and holding a hat, the mother wore a long fur coat. They were standing at the foot of Abraham Lincoln's statue in Springfield, sternly facing the camera. There was a photo of a younger Parkhurst in a naval officer's uniform with ribbons on his chest. When could he have been in the navy? Then she realized it was the father's photograph. They were almost cloned, father and son. Written across the photograph was "For Edward Parkhurst from his father, August 3, 1943." That was almost 50 years ago. How old had the son been? Five? And there was a photograph of his own family before the fireplace in their living room, Parkhurst and his wife expressionless in the center, their children on either side, a large Irish setter seated on its paws in front of them. Each daughter had initials on her sweater, the wife wore a tweed jacket. They were such formal people. Did they all love each other? She wondered. She touched the photograph. Why was he touching her? A framed Order of the Coif, another from his admission to the Supreme Court. She saw a light switch and turned it on. There were several strange pieces of art. A painting of a fiery bird like a hawk caught in a tree, the hawk's wings on fire. A white plaster nude torso of a woman with the eyes made of glittering pieces of glass in mosaic. Beside her on his telephone table was a small sculpture of a red Chicago fireplug that looked like it had melted down. There was a seating area with a television, a VCR, and a stereo with headphones. She imagined Parkhurst in the chair with his eyes closed. She looked at his tapes—Beethoven, Mahler, Mozart, several operas.

She turned the lights off and was about to leave, but just before she left the office she had an impulse to open his desk drawer. She saw it was locked, but she'd seen where he kept the key, in a slim white porcelain Japanese vase. She shook the vase, and the key fell out on to the desk. She opened the drawer. There were several white envelopes, but they were unsealed. She looked in one. It was full of thousand-dollar bills. She counted to twenty. He kept twenty thousand in cash in his desk. She looked in another white envelope. There were five passbooks. She opened one. There was only one entry, of one hundred thousand dollars, in his name. She opened another passbook, same entry, one hundred thousand dollars. She looked through the other three, each had one hundred thousand dollars, all in his name alone. The man had five hundred thousand dollars in savings accounts in his desk and twenty thousand dollars in cash. Why? Why did he need all this money? She looked at the thousand-dollar bills again and put the envelopes back and closed and locked the drawer and put the key back in the vase. Then she quietly shut his door and left his office.

The young associates were still in the library. They looked up at her. One of them raised a finger as if to say hello.

As she rode the bus back to Loomis street she thought about what she had done. I don't understand them. I will never understand them. But I must become one of them. My people have no lawyers. We are alone. I must become one of them. I am tired, very confused and tired. He is touching me, and I am permitting it. She looked out at the black shadows of the buildings, and shook her head.

In the morning at the legal clinic in the basement of the church she met with a woman who was waiting for her in the entrance. The woman had a young child with her, a boy of about five. They walked through the church, to the side door that led to the basement. The woman was silent. Cecelia opened the door to her basement office. Her desk was a card table. There were folding chairs. The floor was bare. She had a few old law books, a set of three-year-old Illinois Revised Statutes, and some booklets from state agencies.

She asked the woman to be seated. The child sat in the woman's lap and stared at Cecelia with his dark eyes. The mother still did not speak.

"I am a student of the law, like a *notario*. If we can help you, I can perhaps find a lawyer."

The mother remained silent.

"You must speak to me, *señora.*"

The woman's eyes filled with tears, and she put her hands around her son and bowed her head.

"Where is your husband, *señora*?"

She shook her head.

"Has the immigration taken him?"

She nodded yes.

"When did this happen? Last night?"

"*Sí.*"

"Has anyone contacted you?"

She shook her head again.

"So you don't know where your husband is? Was he taken from work? If so, they will have him downtown. When did your husband come to this country?"

The woman looked away. She was trying to hide her tears from her son.

"When did your husband come to the States?"

She didn't answer.

"Was it this year?"

"*Sí.*"

"From Mexico?"

"No."

"*Dónde?*"

"El Salvador."

"Is he a *político?*"

"*Sí. Político.*"

"He will be in danger if he returns?"

"He cannot return."

After the woman left, Cecelia called the restaurant and told them she wouldn't be in. Instead she went downtown to see Edward Parkhurst. They were surprised to see her at noon at the law firm. Parkhurst was at lunch and had a 2:00 appointment. His secretary told her he usually took a short nap after lunch, and at 1:50 she would knock on his door. He followed the same routine, except when he was on trial; lunch at the University Club and then a nap until two, when he either had an appointment or opened up his phone again.

Promptly at ten minutes to two, the secretary knocked on his door. She came to the library and smiled at Cecelia. "He'll see you for just a few minutes."

He was sitting on a chair by the stereo with his earphones on. He motioned to the chair across from his. She could feel his gray eyes watching her as she sat down and crossed her legs.

"I'm surprised to see you here, Cecelia. Mary said you wanted to see me."

"Mr. Parkhurst, I want to ask you to help me."

"What kind of help?" He removed the earphones.

"I work at a legal clinic at our church. A woman came in this morning. Her husband was arrested last night by the immigration. They have him downtown in the federal detention center. He is an illegal, from El Salvador. He will be sent back immediately. They will put him on a plane, perhaps today. If he is sent back, she says they will kill him because he is opposed to them politically. He is a *político*. Under the law he should be entitled to remain here under amnesty. He should be granted political amnesty. But I cannot act for him. I am not a lawyer."

"You want me to act as his lawyer?"

"*Sí.*" She unconsciously answered him in Spanish.

"But I am not an immigration lawyer."

"Yes, but you are a lawyer of great experience."

He put the earphones back on and stretched out his legs to another chair and closed his eyes. He was silent, and then he spoke to her with his eyes closed. "You are rather naive, Cecelia. In some respects still almost a child. If you want to be a lawyer, you have to toughen yourself. You have to understand the profession, this office. The way we do things here." His eyes were still closed to the music. "First understand that we do not do pro bono work."

"Our church could perhaps pay a small fee."

He smiled. "No, we don't want money from your church. We simply do not do pro bono work. It is an absolute rule of the firm. Some of the young lawyers do it on their own, but that's their affair. Instead we contribute money. We contribute to all the great charities of Chicago. To the university legal clinics, to the Bar Association legal clinic. In that manner we discharge our responsibility to the community. We simply cannot afford to do pro bono work. What is your client's name?"

"Felipe García."

"The matter of Felipe García would be inextricably lost in our office. It does not belong here. It is simply a matter of efficiency. Cost. We cannot afford to serve the Felipe Garcías of the world. If you are to work with us, you must understand that."

She felt ashamed for having asked him. Her legs were weak, and a hot flush enveloped her body.

He took his earphones off and handed them to her.

"Tchaikovsky. *Swan Lake.* Listen to it, Cecelia." He reached out and carefully placed the earphones over her head. "He was a

very complicated man, Tchaikovsky. Peter Ilyitch." He adjusted
the earphones and touched her hair. The music began to wash over
her. It calmed her for a moment as he stared at her. He took her
hand.

She closed her eyes. He leaned toward her. She could sense his
face moving toward her and now he kissed her, at first lightly, his
lips just brushing hers, and then he parted her lips with his tongue
and slowly moved his tongue into her mouth. He then moved
away from her and held her face in her hands.

"You're a beautiful young woman, Cecelia. But you have much
to learn. We could become friends. If we are to become friends, I
will make an exception for your Mr. Felipe García and I will help
him." He stood her up and took the earphones off and put his
arms around her and held her and pressed himself into her. She
recoiled as he kissed her neck and let her go. "You are a lovely
child. Most complicated and mysterious. But if we are to be
friends, I will help you. I am leaving for Detroit this afternoon, but
I'll take care of the matter before I leave." He held her hands and
then slowly let her go. He put on his vest with its silver chain and
jacket and smoothed his hair and stood in his pinstripe gray suit in
front of a mirror. "Leave his name with Mary," he said.

She went to the law school that evening, and as she sat in her
torts class, her ears were ringing. She really couldn't hear the professor. Parkhurst's tongue inside her mouth was like a fat larva. Not
the black snake she'd seen in a store window, but a fat, slimy larva
that had inserted itself inside the white pulp of a nut and was feeding on the pulp, slowly twisting into the soft meat of the inner
shell. The professor was talking about foreseeability. She stopped
taking notes. Was this the price she had to pay? No. She knew it
was wrong. But she seemed frozen, incapable of striking back. She
was taught to be gentle among men. His tongue felt like slime, like
the swollen worm at the bottom of a mescal bottle. There was a
legend that whoever ate the worm at the bottom of the bottle
would become a real man. *Qué hombre bravo! Qué gringo bastardo!*

She didn't go to work at the law firm after school that night.

Instead she went to the movies. She bought some popcorn and she lost herself in the film. Afterwards, on the bus, she at last felt relaxed. Her ears had stopped ringing, and she tried not to think about the situation. On the back of the seat facing her was some graffiti—Carlos, Jaime, *Las Aguilas*. The Eagles. She traced the diamond shape around the scrawl of *Las Aguilas* and closed her eyes. What would it be like, to soar high above a valley in the mountain winds, to be free and powerful? To be like the eagle. A night hunter. This city was full of night hunters. She would practice law somewhere else, perhaps in a small town in New Mexico, where the darkness was not filled with hunters, where they did not always come at you with their talons ready. All the strange young white men. So sure of themselves. So superior. So confident. The best minds of the country. She shook her long black hair back and stared out the window.

The following morning when she went to the legal aid office in the church, the woman was already waiting for her, seated with her son in the lobby.

Cecelia asked if her husband had been released.

The woman shook her head. Cecelia could see the woman's face was streaked with tears.

"*Señora*, he will be today. I am very confident."

The woman shook her head again.

"What is it, *señora?*"

"He is gone. They have taken him."

"No. There must be a mistake."

The little boy stared at Cecelia innocently and poked one finger up his nose.

The woman held out a wrinkled piece of paper. The child wandered into the church and began running down the aisle toward the altar. Cecelia took the woman's paper. It was a telegram in English:

The Department of Immigration informs you that Felipe García has been transported by air to his place of origin, El Salvador, effective hour 1930 this date.

Cecelia held her arms out to the woman. The boy came skipping back down the aisle. He had a red wax flower that he had taken from the altar, and he held it as he watched his mother cry.

That evening when Cecelia returned to the office, there was a sense of excitement. Tomorrow was the Simeon McCutcheon Memorial Track Meet, and all the contestants had been given commemorative T-shirts printed on the reverse side with a black silkscreen of the deceased senior partner of the McCutcheon firm. He had founded the track meet twenty years ago.

When she saw Parkhurst, he was already wearing one of the T-shirts over his sweatshirt. He had a green and white stocking cap on and his sweats with green shorts over them, and his feet up on his desk.

"Hello, Cecelia. We'll be outside tonight. I want you to clock us in at the Art Institute. I've even brought a piece of tape so we can simulate finishes."

"Mr. Parkhurst, what have you done for Felipe García?"

"Oh my God, Cecelia, I forgot about García." He sat back and took his feet off his desk and looked at his watch. "It's too late to do anything tonight. I just had so much to wind down in Detroit, some very complex negotiations. I have a friend on the board of Travelers Aid. He has some immigration experience. I'll call him tomorrow."

She didn't answer him.

"I'll take care of it. I promise you."

She looked at him without speaking, but as he reached out for her hand, she turned her back on him and walked back to the library.

That night she stood alone in a light snowfall with a stopwatch behind the north lion of the Art Institute. It was bitterly cold, and the city seemed to be made out of ice. Her gloves were too thin, and she could barely see down Michigan Avenue because the wind kept blowing drifts of snow. The snow seemed to come at her like the white wings of eagles, drifting in patterns through the lights. She thought she could look up through the buildings and see the

large white birds sailing. She had the stopwatch and the finish
tape, a piece of clothesline Parkhurst had given her. She tied it to a
young tree planted at the curb in front of the entrance. Then she
took the rope and walked it back to the stairs and pulled it taut,
testing it. If she held it tightly, tied to the young tree, and pulled it
taut, aimed at the runner's throat at the exact moment of the
impact of the runner, it would probably kill him. It would be so
easy. She practiced with the rope and pulled it taut as steel, then
dropped it to lay hidden in the soft snow on the walk.

The runners were coming now. She could see them mixing in
the colors of the lights. They were a block away. Which one was
Parkhurst? She squinted and looked for the green stocking cap. She
had to be sure. She didn't want to injure anyone, just Parkhurst.
Right at the throat, his arms spread, those silly shorts. They were
coming now. What a surprise it would be. I am waiting for you.
She smiled. They were thirty yards away. Jeremy was in the lead,
striding gracefully and easily, only a few yards separating the runners. The snow made them seem like figures running in a glass
ball, all suspended in place. Jeremy reached his arms out. She
counted and watched, holding the rope slack in the snow with
both hands just below her waist. Now Stephen and then Peter,
Tom, and now Parkhurst. She began to cry. He was coming so
clearly now, so open and unprepared, the thin white neck, the
arrogant face. Her hand tensed, and she pulled the rope taut as his
body hit it, but she let go and dropped the rope in the snow. He
passed through, foolishly exultant, only feeling the light touch
against his throat.

The next night at a dinner at the Hilton in honor of the track
meet, Cecelia was a guest. The team had won first prize and they
were all very drunk. She sat between Parkhurst and Jeremy, across
from a table laden with champagne and hors d'oeuvres and topped
by a large horse sculpted in ice. As the men drank their champagne, Peter challenged each of them to climb the table to the top
of the ice horse. He went first, and barely held on, then rolled off
into the shrimp salad. Parkhurst then tried and fell off immediate-

ly, and so did Stephen and Tom. Only Jeremy remained with her at the table. They were all on the floor laughing and covered with food, and squirting champagne.

"I don't want to try," Jeremy called down to them.

Then Cecelia, in her ruffled silk dress, stood up. She got up on the table and climbed to the level of the ice horse. She looked down at each of them, and silently, gracefully, with almost no effort, ascended the ice horse and mounted it, wrapped her legs around it, and held her back very stiffly, and put one hand up. She sat there for a minute and then got down, and without saying anything, found her coat and left them forever.

Ash

I T HAD BEGUN with a jade flower. He had spent two weeks last year in Japan and had brought back a small jade flower for his desk and later he transferred it to his bench. He found solace in the flower as he listened to the lawyers' arguments. He used it as a secret worry stone, holding its smooth jade petals between his thumb and forefinger under the bench. It was as if the jade flower had become a kind of touchstone for him, and touching it brought him relief from all the fury swirling around him.

He had been a giant in Japan, a tall African-American man striding down the street. People would stare at him and then turn around. Often they would bow in solemn greeting as he passed. He'd gone to a tea house and the geisha who served him had slowly touched his hand, brushing it with her fingers to see if his color would come off. He had also touched her face with his finger and traced the configuration of her eyebrows and the red slash of her lips. It was then that she reached into her kimono and had given him the jade flower as a gift.

He was a judge in the Domestic Relations of the Circuit Court of Cook County. His name was Arthur Williams, Jr. He was a tall man, with the athletic grace of the runner he'd been in college. He had the handsome face of an ancient tribe of African warriors, with angry, dark eyes that made him seem remote or detached, as if he had an inner secret life, that, like the flower, was kept from you but secretly sustained him. He had high angular cheekbones and his

hair, at 50, was slightly balding and had gone gray along his temples. Apart from the remoteness, he came at you as a very strong
self-assured man, but always there seemed to be a touch of
repressed anger.

It was rumored for the last two years that he was about to be
selected for the Appellate Court and then picked for the next
vacancy in the U. S. District Court, but the nomination hadn't
come, and he wasn't certain any more that it would ever come. He
was tired of thinking about it. The politics of the appointment
were very intricate. There were a lot of people to please. He'd spent
most of his life pleasing these people.

He'd begun his career twenty-five years ago in Traffic Court,
and then been moved to 11th and State to Gun Court. He'd never
erased the memory of the gray light of the morning call in Gun
Court, the men, almost always black, in cuffs as they were brought
out of the holding cell, blinking at the light, quickly searching for
relatives in the courtroom, the stench of the place, the shuffling
lines of defendants. Then he was a Public Defender at 26th and
California for four years, working his way up on felony cases to the
defense of murder cases. He was transferred to the Appellate
Division of the Defender's office and he became a good brief
writer. The First Assistant soon named him "The Scholar." Then,
he was transferred back to the prosecutor's office and he prosecuted
armed robbery and rapes, and finally murder cases. After four years
of that he became Chief of a prosecutor team and then he was slated for judge.

After he was appointed judge, he went back on almost the
same circuit. First he was sent to Traffic Court, then to 11th and
State, then Juvenile, and for three years he heard personal injury
cases in the Law Division and then sat in the Criminal Court for
several years. Now for three years he'd been in the Divorce
Division. He seldom complained. He had a good reputation and
he was a tough judge. He always tried to avoid the job requests and
the thousand favors that he was asked. They were viewed as just
small favors, and none of them had ever stuck to him because he

was talented at avoiding most of them. He learned to make people feel that he had helped them when he hadn't done anything to help them. The people passed through the seine of his courtroom like tiny silver fish and he never became involved with them. He remained detached and aloof. He kept his skills as a scholar. He tried to stay abreast of the law and he was active in the Bar Associations. He attended seminars. He always worked hard.

His only real failure had been his marriage. He was divorced when he was in his mid-30's and never remarried. There were no children, and although he now had one special woman friend, from what he learned from the pain of his own divorce and had seen in the Divorce Court, he had no desire to remarry. He'd been married to a lawyer he'd met when she was in the Public Defender's office. She was now working for a firm in Los Angeles, the only black woman in their firm. Their marriage had been a mistake, they were too competitive and it lasted two years. He liked the freedom of being single, the opportunity to travel, to meet new people.

On the trip to Japan last year, he met John Wakefield. Wakefield was a partner in one of Chicago's largest firms. He met John Wakefield and his wife on the JAL flight going over and they saw each other several times during the trip. Since his return he received invitations from the Wakefields for dinner and had occasionally met John Wakefield at John's club.

He had always been cautious of white men and their clubs. He felt he never really was welcome. It also made him feel uncomfortable to be served by black waiters and usually he was the only black person seated as a guest in the room. Over the years he'd also learned to be distrustful of the big law firms.

He was raised as an only child in Alabama where his father had a small farm and later, after he died, his mother lost it. They came to live with his aunt in Chicago and his mother worked as a domestic. In high school he'd stayed out of the street gangs and won a partial scholarship to Howard University. When he went back south to college, his mother died. She never lived to see him become a lawyer. He returned to Chicago with a grant to John Marshall Law School and got a part time day job as a guard in an office building and a night job at the post office. Even with this work schedule he was in the top ten per cent of his class.

After graduation there were no jobs for him or any other black graduates of John Marshall at any of Chicago' large law firms, so with the help of his alderman, now the ward committeeman, he was offered a job with the States Attorney's office. Time and again, Chicago's large law firms turned him down, many of them refusing even an interview. He knew that things hadn't changed that much since his graduation. Of the seven black men who had been in the law school only two were practicing law. One had become a crack head, one had become a real estate broker, two were working for Internal Revenue. One man had disappeared. The one black woman graduate had become an administrator with the Board of Education.

Recently some of these firms had begun to move into divorce and establish divorce departments, like they'd begun bankruptcy departments. Divorce and bankruptcy were now considered lucrative new profit centers. The fees were often very large. Lawyers from the firms had begun to appear in his courtroom, usually representing executives and their wives, the male lawyers in neat grey suits, the young women lawyers in black stockings and dark suits. Then soon following them came their fee petitions. "Courtesy copies" of the Petitions were always sent to him in advance of the hearings. It was all very corporate and orderly, all hours accounted for, Lexis and Westlaw expenses tabulated. Partners were billed at $150 to $250 per hour and associates at $95 to $150. Apparently dissolution of the marriages of corporate managers was just another cost of doing business, like moving expenses. He presided over these proceedings, usually in his chambers, very seldom in open court.

He lived alone in a one-bedroom apartment in a glass high-rise building on Randolph Street near the Lake, and each morning he'd walk to his courtroom. Most days he'd be out of his building at six and he'd jog in Grant Park, sometimes with his friend, a lovely divorced African-American woman in her 30's who was in advertising and who lived two blocks from him. She had become his special friend. Often they jogged together through the park to Michigan Avenue and then past the Art Institute to Jackson, and across to Buckingham Fountain and cut across the park and back to their apartments. He with a Michael Jordan headband, she in a purple jogging outfit. In the springtime, before their run, they did stretching exercises near the bed of spring flowers that had been planted, and in the summer they'd stop and watch the early tennis players. After running, he'd shower, shave, have coffee and a roll and his first cigarette and walk briskly to his courtroom. If she stayed over they'd walk to Michigan Avenue together. Usually he'd stop for no one, nodding to lawyers who recognized him, always pleasant but reserved. He wasn't a handshaker, a backslapper. He wasn't a pol. He was a serious man of high purpose and carried himself that way, eyes straight ahead, not lingering with ward politicians who tried to approach him in the lobby of the Daley Center. When he got to his floor he'd quickly cut through the crowd of people standing in the corridor or sitting on the radiators, young women and their husbands sitting far apart from each other, children, grandmothers, witnesses, lawyers arguing in the hall, bored clerks with armloads of files. He'd push through them into the sanctuary of the coated glass Judge's entrance that led to his chambers.

Recently, though, in the early days of spring, he'd become transfixed with the beggars he passed on his walk to the Daley Center each morning. Now that winter was over, like grey birds returning, the beggars had suddenly appeared again. They were on the edge of the park and at the intersections. Most of them were black men. One man on crutches under Marshall Field's clock had only stubs for hands, a face that had been severely scarred and seared by burns, a puckered mouth like a paralyzed clown with purple lips. This man would look up at him and mutter. He would drop a dollar into the man's hat at his feet. There was an older

black man with a sweet smile and stumps for teeth who carried a
trumpet in an open case and often sat in the sunlight on a metal
box at Michigan and Randolph. Another black man always stood
under an awning at Wabash. He danced in spasms. He was blind
and sang and writhed and shook his cup. Another man was paralyzed from a stroke and could barely stand. This man was usually
slumped up against the wall of the library holding his cup. "Thank
you, man," he always said to the judge. "Thank you, man." Once
he'd said, "Pull up my pants, man." His trousers were falling and
with his paralyzed hands he couldn't pull them up, so he helped
him. He had immediately washed his hands as soon as he got to
his chambers.

He tried to avoid them, all the black hands reaching up to
him, their wounded eyes like dying animals. Occasionally there
was a white beggar, a muttering, angry, thin, little woman in a tattered cloth coat in front of St. Peter's, or a wild drunk defecating in
his trousers, lurching on Madison Street, but the beggars were
mostly black. The rattle of their cups and their moaning had
become a sad threnody that stayed with him now and wouldn't
leave him even as his morning call began. He would hear that
strange syncopation of the sounds of the coins rattling in the cups
and the moans and chants. The sounds began as soon as the
lawyers approached his bench with the call of the first case. He'd
imperceptively shake his head to get the sad music out of his mind
and secretly reach for the jade flower.

These last weeks he'd taken the bus to work and the sounds of
the beggars had diminished. He was hearing a case involving mil-
lions of dollars in property and he wanted to try to discipline himself and become interested in it. Chicago had become a kind of
Calcutta of street people, and he knew his daily dollars weren't
going to make the difference.

John Wakefield's firm was trying the case of Mithun vs.
Mithun in his courtroom. Richard Mithun was the president of
one of Chicago's largest corporations and was Wakefield's personal
client. Mithun wanted to leave his wife of ten years to marry a

younger woman. His wife had signed a premarital agreement and had agreed to a settlement in the event of a divorce. Her lawyers argued that the prenuptial agreement was invalid because Mithun had failed to disclose ownership of certain stock options which would have tripled his net worth. Mithun had exercised the options during the marriage. They argued that the non-disclosure of the stock options made the prenuptial agreement invalid.

He knew that the prenuptial agreement was invalid and Mithun's failure to disclose the stock options was a fraud on the wife .

Two weeks ago he and his friend had been invited to dinner at the Wakefield's apartment. He thought of cancelling the dinner because the Mithun case was coming up for trial. He even thought of recusing himself from Mithun because of his friendship with Wakefield but if he recused himself from every case when he knew a lawyer, he'd have to strip himself of most of his cases. He felt that Wakefield would be sensitive to his position and wouldn't bring up Mithun. Also he liked to play mind games with these powerful white lawyers. He liked to match himself against them. After dinner in the elegant dining room overlooking Lake Michigan the women excused themselves and the two men had cognac together and then stood watching the traffic.

Wakefield had a lean, patrician face. His only nervous mannerism was a tic at the corner of his mouth that made him seem to occasionally grimace. He was raised in Winnetka and had gone to the University of Chicago Law School. He was a strange combination of ivory tower elitist and rainmaker. His wife was petulant and neurotic and this evening wore a lavender sari and drank excessively.

"Art, I understand Cam Smith will be up before you in two weeks on Mithun. How's he doing on the case?"

"Cam Smith is a good trial lawyer. He always handles himself well."

"Apparently the woman signed a perfectly valid prenuptial agreement." Wakefield cradled his cognac and stirred it and smiled, a slight smile. He didn't answer him. He wouldn't give him the satisfaction of an answer. Wakefield hunched his shoulders and put his glass down. "Enough said. I know you can't talk about pending matters and I would never want to put you on the spot, Arthur, particularly with all this Greylord thing that's hanging over the courts. You know Arthur, I consider you an old friend after the good times we had together in Japan. I think both of us trust each other." His eyes flashed. He touched the judge on the back and they walked toward the stairway together and nothing more was said.

T HIS MORNING after two days of trial he would rule on Mithun. After he got off the bus and took the elevator up to his chambers he could smell cigar smoke in his office. Bill Simpkins was sitting there, the wily old man who had been the boss of Arthur Williams' ward for thirty years. As alderman, Bill Simpkins had gotten Arthur Williams his appointment as state's attorney and finally the appointment as judge. Simpkins had suffered a stroke and his face was now yellow and seamed, heavy lidded, his thin hair white. He wore dark glasses and looked very frail. Simpkins had never visited Arthur Williams in chambers. This was the first time.

The judge closed his door and Simpkins' face broke into a jagged smile and he shook his head as if he was reaffirming their old friendship.

"Arthur, how are you?"

"Bill, I'm fine."

The old man nodded his head again and squinted at a spot of sunlight that came through the blinds. The judge went over and closed them. "No, don't bother, Arthur. I like the sun on my face."

"I haven't seen you in a year, Bill. Not since the ward dinner at the Hilton."

"That was a great fundraiser, Arthur." The old committeeman looked at him carefully but didn't change expression. He cleared his throat, spit into a handkerchief, sighed and tapped the ash from his cigar.

"You've always been your own man, Arthur. I'm not a man to put one of my judges on the spot. But it's not illegal for a judge to accept a campaign contribution so long as it's only a thousand dollars per person, is it? You know a lawyer named Wakefield? He says he's a good friend of yours. I've known him for years. His firm does a lot of condemnation work. I've worked with them before. Wakefield's law office has asked me to deliver a contribution to the Arthur Williams Campaign Fund for Appellate Court Judge." He smiled over his glasses. "Yes, that's right, Arthur Williams, Appellate Court Judge. You heard me. You've finally been slated, Arthur, just this week. So, this fellow Wakefield wants to make a contribution. It's still a free country, even with all these FBI men crawlin' all over the courts like cockroaches. They don't scare me. I'm too old to be scared. Law firms always are contactin' me with contributions, zoning changes, state contracts. You think things have changed? Some things never change."

"I can't accept it, Bill. They have a case in front of me. I'm going to rule on it this morning. Did they tell you that?"

"You don't have to take it. I'll take it. No one's saying anything about your taking anything or asking any favors of you. They didn't say anything about any case. I'm talkin' simply a campaign contribution made to me. It doesn't do any good to buck these powerful lawyers. I learned that long ago. They can help you or they can break you bad. They can bury you in the Divorce Division for the rest of your life. So don't be too quick about this, Arthur."

"Bill, I'm a dead man here. I'm losing my grip as a lawyer, as a person. I'm just a servant to these crazy rich people. I can't stand listening to them any more. Arguing about silverware, paintings, clothes, winter homes, summer homes, boats. Do you think I give a shit about any of this any more after three years of listening to this crap?—But let me tell you, Bill, I'm not going to take their money. I never have, and I never will. If you can't understand that, then after all these years, even you don't really know me. You've been like a father to me, but Bill you have to understand me. These men are just using you."

"Arthur, your next step after the Appellate Court is Federal court. You think of me as a father? I think of you like a son. I don't want a son of mine to lose an appointment he's been waiting on all his life. You cross these men once and you're through. This is still Chicago. Remember, I won't always be around to protect you. I'm old and I'm sick and now I'm spitting blood. I can't hear you talkin' to me like this. Not a son of mine. I don't even hear you. You put those robes on and remember where you came from and who you are. You got an obligation to all your people to go on the Federal court. Once you get there, you can be as high and mighty as you want. But until you're there, you play the game the way it's always been played, or else you could be sitting in Divorce the rest of your life. I'm not goin' to fight with you, Arthur. I said my piece."

The old man stood up and took both of the judge's hands.

He looked for his cane. "See, Arthur? I'm usin' a cane now and I forgot where I put it. I'm an old man now and I forget. Time passes so quickly you don't even hear it."

The old ward committeeman slowly left the judge's office and tossed the Wakefields firm's envelope on the desk. The judge locked his door and sat back and slit open the envelope. There were twenty-five $1,000 checks neatly made out to The Judge Arthur Williams, Jr. Campaign Fund from twenty-five separate lawyers, each of them with the name of the individual attorney's limited partnership. There were also two $1,000 bills with yellow "Post-It" stickers on them. Each had the legend "Anonymous." There was $27,000 in the envelope, $25,000 in checks and $2,000 in cash.

He took the two $1,000 notes out. He couldn't remember ever having seen a $1,000 bill. He had his opinion ready. He could just tear up the opinion, cash the bills, break them into $100s, walk the city streets and hand them out to all the beggars.

It was all so neat and corporate, so dignified. The perfectly typed, perforated checks, even the typography on the labels was perfect, yet it was so arrogant. Did they really think they could make a campaign contribution to him. It was ludicrous to send

Simpkins to him on the day of his ruling as their messenger. It wasn't even ludicrous, it was unbelievable and showed the depth of their contempt for him and his Court. Did they think they were so powerful that they were immune? How did they know he wouldn't report them? Some of the Greylord defendants had been indicted for the same kind of thing. Why didn't they just stuff his pockets with money or leave it in his desk drawer or pay off his bank loan. "Anonymous" was such a strange word. What did it mean? That the person using the word didn't exist? That the hand behind the word wasn't a human hand? It was a person's hand, though, that he knew, and he took his hand and held one of the bills up, picked up his desk lighter and lit a cigarette. He should stop smoking. He also knew that. His hand was trembling. He took the first $1,000 bill and stared at it and then touched at its corner with the flame of his lighter and held it up and watched it crumble into flame and disappear into a fine charred grey ash on his ashtray. Now the hand that had sent the money was no longer anonymous. The money didn't exist, so the hand didn't exist. Was it a violation of Federal law to burn a thousand dollar bill? If so, who would bring the charge?

He took the second bill, held it up to the flame and watched it burn into ash. He did the same thing with all the checks. He put them in a stack and held them over his large circular glass ashtray touched them with the flame and let them burn until they crumbled into a pile of ash.

He slowly put on his robes and sat down in his judge's chair, a high brass-studded leather chair, and swivelled to the mirror in back of him. He was still a dignified looking man, wasn't he? He had a very dark face in the mirror and now his finger touched at it with some of the grey ash. First his eyes. He touched his eyelids grey. Now the broad forehead. He daubed it with the charred ash, streaked it with grey ash. He looked like a Masai chieftain, his face covered in ash before a ceremony of battle. A few traces along his cheek. He took the rest of the ash and swept it back into Wakefield's envelope and sealed it.

Then he walked out of his chambers into the corridor. His secretary heard him but didn't look up and sounded a buzzer in the courtroom. He stood for a moment and composed himself. His hands were still trembling. He walked into the courtroom. The bailiff immediately rapped. The clerk read the morning call from a piece of cardboard. "Everyone rise...hear ye, hear ye, hear ye, this Honorable Court of the Circuit Court of Cook County, is now in session, the Honorable Arthur Williams, Jr. presiding. Please be seated and remain quiet." The bailiff sounded the gavel.

He sat down behind the bench and smiled briefly at the lawyers.

"Good morning, ladies and gentlemen..."

"Mithun vs. Mithun," the clerk called out.

Two groups of lawyers came forward to the bench. They were immaculately dressed. They all looked alike to him. "Like little squirrels," someone had once said. "They look like very expensive grey squirrels." Fresh faces, pleasant smiles. It was as if they were in a church and he was their pastor. He could place his hands over them and absolve them all, himself, the court, all with a simple gesture. The courtroom wall bore the legend, "In God We Trust." That was what it was all about, wasn't it. Absolution. That's all they asked of him. He heard the sad music coming up at him again. If they had noticed the streaks of grey ash on his face, no one dared say anything.

He cleared his throat and slowly put on his glasses, hooking one frame at a time over his ears. He was very angry and yet he controlled his voice. He spoke quietly. "In Mithun vs. Mithun, I've ruled on this issue of the stock options in a written opinion. My clerk will have copies for all of you. Let me just say that I've ruled in favor of Mrs. Mithun. I'm going to grant her petition to set aside the prenuptial agreement as fraudulent because of the failure of Mr. Mithun to disclose the stock options."

He stared at the lawyers.

Mrs. Mithun's lawyers began congratulating themselves. Wakefield's team was grim, particularly the lead attorney, Cameron Smith, who was shaking his head.

"Mr. Smith, if you'll see me in chambers for a minute, I think I still have one of your exhibits." The judge stood and walked back to his chambers. The bailiff sounded his gavel again and Smith followed the judge.

He closed the door and glanced at himself in the mirror again. He did look like a Masai chieftain. He smiled. Smith stood in front of him. The lawyer's mouth was set in a thin line and he didn't speak. He looked down at the remnant of ash on the desk.

"I have an envelope for you, Mr. Smith. I received it from your Mr. Wakefield. So I'm returning it to both of you." He handed Smith the sealed envelope. The lawyer stared at him, began to say something and then didn't, and turned and quickly left.

He looked at his face in the mirror again and rubbed some of the ash into his forehead with the heel of his hand. He didn't need them. His pension was vested. He'd spent twenty-five years in the system trying to please them and now he would leave before he became just another fool. A geisha. His face was almost grey with ash, but he could still wash if off. He wasn't going to clean toilets for them at a federal penitentiary. His mother had done enough of that. Maybe he would volunteer for the Peace Corps and go to Africa and become a teacher. Maybe they would back off now. These were dangerous times to be putting heat on a judge. May be they would back off. He doubted it.

Casimir Zymak

THERE WAS A little tavern that I remember on California Avenue near the Criminal Court where they served blood red Polish sausages from a huge communal jar while you played "bumper pool" and people passing on the streets would pause by the tavern window and watch your game. That is the place, "Anton's Tavern," that is freshest in my memory. And when I think about my friend Casimir Zymak, I remember him best at "Anton's" by the pool table, standing there with cue stick in hand, very formally turning to you with a bow and a smile, drinking his cognac down, his tiny eyes glistening with pleasure.

Casimir Zymak was perhaps a great criminal lawyer. Few members of the Chicago Bar remember him other than as a drunken old man, lurching through the courthouse corridors, muttering and cursing to himself. He was so pathetic, perhaps even mad, that those of us who had known him and admired him grew afraid of him and abandoned him. Occasionally a friend would slip a ten or a twenty into his pocket and try to talk to him about the old days, but Zymak would stumble away like a punch drunk fighter.

In his last days before his death, his skin yellowed and grew taut on his face, and where once smile lines had etched the eyes and corners of his mouth, the skin cracked into overlays. His clothes grew filthy and his teeth rotted. He spent his last few months hanging around the Traffic Court, trying to cadge fifty dollar cases. Zymak, who had tried more than one hundred murder cases and had been one of the defense Bar's most courageous and skillful practitioners, was then brought before the Chicago Bar Association to answer a disbarment proceeding. Fortunately, death intervened and the proceeding was dismissed. I remember his funeral procession. On the way to the cemetery the cortege passed the Criminal Court Building and the hearse stopped for a moment of tribute. I think he would have liked that. He was, in many ways, a curiously formal man. He believed in rite and ceremony and he would have regarded the stopping of the hearse as proper and not maudlin.

I believe I first met Zymak in 1954 or 1955. I had been just admitted to the Bar and was working for a firm that had a very broad general practice, including some criminal defense work. Occasionally, I was sent out to the Criminal Court at 26th and California to argue some minor motion. Often, I'd stop at "Anton's" and have a beer and sausage sandwich for lunch. It was a friendly neighborhood tavern. Anton was a fat, bald ex-cop with a loud voice who would run a tab on a young lawyer graciously and with the same coarse humor that he reserved for the cash customers. He thought nothing of bellowing out, "Hey, fat ass," to a friend in the crowd at his bar, mostly minor pols from the court building, bailiffs, stenos, defense lawyers and a few cops. It was a good crowd and if you lingered over your beer or cognac long enough into the afternoon, there would always be plenty of action in the back booths where the shadows fell.

Out of these shadows, late one afternoon, stepped Casimir Zymak, lipstick smeared across his face, flushed and excited, drink in hand, a rather fat, older woman blowing kisses to him from one of the booths. I was introduced to him as a young lawyer who had just passed the Bar examination. I remember that he was very grave and rigid despite the lipstick smears. He shook my hand and smiled and told me that I had chosen an honorable profession, the greatest of all for service to my fellow man. "But one word of advice...young man...get yourself a jockey. Right off...get yourself a jockey or you'll never be a success." With those words, he ruffled my hair, clapped me on the back and went back to the booth and the fat lady and a round of fresh drinks.

Some months later, I learned what Zymak had meant when he told me to "get myself a jockey." He meant a "runner" someone who would chase after cases and deliver clients to the lawyer for a percentage of the fee. I had thought that "ambulance chasing" was a practice limited to certain members of the personal injury Bar, but I soon learned that many of the criminal lawyers I met employed "runners".

Very often, the "runner" would also be the lawyer's banker. Sometimes the "runner" would virtually own the lawyer. The lawyer would borrow from his man or fail to pay him his full cut on a case and soon the lawyer would only be working to pay off his jockey. It was typical of Zymak that when we first met he would tell me in a loud voice to go out and "get myself a jockey". He had contempt for the score of "runners" that he owed, many of whom hung around "Anton's", and in his own way he liked to defy them. He knew though that the jockey would end up riding the man.

Zymak was ridden principally by a jockey named "Petey." He had other jockeys all looking for a cut of the action, but "Petey" was his principal jockey.

Petey was a short, fat, pop-eyed little Greek with a flushed face and a long nose. He was also very good with his belly. He and Zymak would stroll into the saloon about four in the afternoon, Petey always waddling a few steps ahead, and Petey would move up to the bar and stick his belly out and yell "Fill'er up, you foul mouthed Polack." It was a routine. Everyone would laugh and Anton would snort, "The Greek's here, cover up behind, all you finks, watch the lousy Greek." Then Zymak would come up to the bar, nodding his way with curt, serious greetings, shaking hands limply with friends.

After Zymak's death, I lost touch with Petey. I heard though that he had trouble finding himself another man and that he hung around the tracks a lot, running bets and touting. Maybe Petey had always dreamed of becoming a real jock, but by then he was too old and too sad. When Zymak went down, they say he was into Petey for twenty grand.

The last time I saw Petey was in a little Greek grocery store out on Harrison Street down the block from the Kringas-Marzullo funeral home. I'd been to a wake and afterwards stopped in the grocery to buy some bread, cheese and black olives for a midnight snack. Petey was playing cards with some old men at a table at the rear of the store next to the freezer where the racks of lamb were hanging ready for the Easter customers. He saw me and gave me a wink but he didn't get up to say hello. He was very thin and when he looked at me, I knew I made him remember Zymak, so I just paid for the groceries and left without going over to him. A lost jock, without a mount, his colors struck, I've never seen him again.

In addition to Petey the "runner", Zymak was always accompanied by a bodyguard, a man named Rettig. Rettig didn't have all his marbles. A great, ham-fisted, square headed man, his eyes shone with docile madness. He was always in and out of Chicago State, and when he was out, he was with Zymak. He was the kind of man who would wear a white hoodlum's fedora perched on the top of his huge head and stand around, his tongue catching the spittle ebbing from a corner of his mouth. Rettig was built like a pro tackle but couldn't be trusted to return with change from a cigar stand. He was just there, always ready at Zymak's side. I was told that Rettig wasn't really Zymak's bodyguard. That many years ago, after Rettig's mother had died, Zymak had himself appointed as Rettig's conservator. Rettig had been left a small income from a six flat on Thomas Street and Zymak handled the money and gave Rettig an allowance. Anyway, when I met Zymak, he and Rettig were living together in the six flat on Thomas Street. Rettig slept in the back sun parlor and kept house, washing Zymak's socks and in the mornings, frying bacon and eggs. I remember picking Zymak up, on the way to court, and there would be Rettig in his Fedora and underwear, bent over the stove. I always stayed out on the porch because I was afraid of taking the big fellow by surprise.

Zymak's wife had divorced him early in his career and Rettig, although a poor substitute for a good wife, was regarded by Zymak as a much better deal than the former Mrs. Zymak. Whenever Rettig had a spell and became unmanageable, Zymak would move out and call the cops to take him back to Chicago State. Then with Rettig in the hospital, Zymak would move in with Petey or just sleep in the office. When Zymak died, I was told that Rettig was put away for good. Rettig too had probably lost a bundle on Zymak, but he never knew it and had he known, the huge body-guard would have been beyond sadness.

Casimir Zymak was a Pole. He had a round face, high cheek-bones, a ruddy complexion, it was a very mobile face. When he was lost in thought, his forehead would crinkle into pensive lines. When he laughed, his face would shine with delight. He was a young man in appearance, although when I met him he was already in his mid-fifties and died before reaching sixty. His hair remained untouched by gray, a flaxen color, fine and closely cut and his voice was deep and strong and richly accented. He was a short, solid looking man. He had the appearance of being strong and assured, always looking to me like a mill hand or tool and die maker dressed for a Sunday outing. When you shook his hand you would expect to feel the hand of a working man, but his hand was as smooth as an old stone.

Zymak and I became friends, largely because I enjoyed shoot-ing pool. Many afternoons we would shoot pool at "Anton's", while waiting for his jury to come out with a verdict. He would lecture me on points of law. He enjoyed our discussions as much as I did and it gave him someone to talk to other than Petey and Rettig.

He was a good pool shot. He liked to shoot with a cigarette hanging from his lips and squint at the shot through the smoke. Then he'd place his hand in a careful bridge and slowly aim the shot, drawing his cue, back and forth, back and forth until he stroked. It was great relaxation for him. We became good friends. I was his pool playing friend and student. He was my professor. After the games, often we'd break for a sandwich or a glass of wine. If his case was going well, he'd be in an expansive mood and ask Anton to mix up a punch bowl cocktail that was mixed with Southern Comfort as its base and colored with grenadine. Anton served these drinks in thin-stemmed, fragile glasses he reserved for Zymak's special cocktail. Petey, Rettig, Zymak and I would retire to a table and Anton would bring the drinks through the crowd, carrying them high on a platter, and serving us with serious dignity. Then Zymak would toast us all and talk about how after his case he would head for the Wisconsin lake country. He always pronounced it "Visconsin". There, in "Visconsin", by a lake, he would get away to relax and enjoy the sun and the clear air. It was always his dream "to take a little holiday," and I was to be his traveling companion.

After I had known Zymak for about one year, he asked me to help him with some of his cases. If he had a point he wanted researched or a motion to type that involved a legal argument, I'd work in his office after hours. The next morning, before court, I'd leave the papers for him.

Then one night he threw a murder indictment on the desk and asked me to assist him in the trial. I had never seen an indictment before. Zymak had been carrying the document around with him for several days. It was crumpled and worn, stapled in a blue cover, with a half moon of a coffee cup staining the first page. Zymak put his glasses on, down forward on his nose, and in a quiet, formal voice read the indictment to me.

I did help him with the case. The defendant was a young man from Texas who had been charged with the murder of his wife. After an extensive trial, he was found guilty by a jury and was sentenced to life imprisonment. The jury had been qualified by the prosecution to render a verdict of death by electrocution. Zymak had no defense to the murder charge, but he saved the young man's life by asking the jury for mercy. I remember he spoke to them about the plea made to Pontius Pilate to give mercy to Christ.

I only remember fragments of the trial. The blue prison-made suit of the defendant and his maroon tie. The way the defendant would get down on his haunches in the prisoner's cell, as we interviewed him, he would smoke and look up at us and then blow the smoke down through his cupped hand holding the cigarette. His fingers were stained heavily from nicotine. Occasionally he would grunt a few words to us, but he wasn't at all verbal and had little to say in his defense except that he refused to admit his guilt. He killed his wife because he was drunk. She had been running around with other men, and one day after drinking all afternoon he killed her in a drunken rage. He told us that he just didn't remember what happened. It wasn't a novel case and the young man had no apology or remorse for his action. So he hunkered down in the prisoner's cell and traced intricate patterns with a forefinger on the damp floor and listened as we plotted out strategy. There were no witnesses to the killing. The State's case was entirely circumstantial. They had the neighbor woman downstairs who heard screaming and shots and heard the dying wife calling her husband's name in wild shrieks. The prosecution found the gun next to the body and traced it to the defendant's ownership. Witnesses were produced who testified to other violent arguments between the young couple. Friends of the girl testified that she had long feared for her life. One of the bartenders at a tavern where the young man had been served testified that the defendant had shown him the gun on the afternoon of the shooting and told him that he was going to kill his wife.

Zymak had no defense to this testimony except skillful cross examination. We had a list of the State's witnesses that had been given to us with the indictment. We went over the list with the defendant in the prisoner's lockup and asked him about the witnesses and what they would say. He would try to tell us and Zymak would listen and determine points for cross examination and discuss them with me. Then the young man would look up and ask us, "Do I have a chance?" or "How's it goin'?" Zymak would reassure him always.

I remember the highbacked, leather counsel chairs. The murder weapon, a pistol, tagged and marked as an exhibit with a red cardboard tag. One of the prosecutors, playing with the gun in front of the jury, twirling the empty chamber on its sprocket and testing the tension of the trigger. The bullets were referred to by Zymak as "pellets" and were all tagged with similar red tags, and placed on the prosecutor's table. I remember after the end of each day's session, walking down the long, empty halls of the Criminal Court building and out the main entrance into darkness, the sudden feeling of relief to be out in the night air and the surprise of neon light and movement on the streets. In the morning, coming into the building, coffee from the blind vendor's stand at the right of the elevators. The sound of cell doors closing and the rattle of keys as the defendant was brought into the courtroom. Bailiffs in blue jackets, coats open, showing side arms. Families sitting on the back benches of the courtroom, waiting for the morning trial call, sitting solemn and frightened. The morning call of cases and the prisoners brought from the lockup, unshaven, pale, shuffling to the bench for continuances. Police officers dressed in blue sweaters sitting in the first few rows. The way the jurors averted their eyes from the defendant when they returned to the courtroom after their deliberation.

After the jury came in with the verdict of guilty, Zymak and I returned to "Anton's" and met Rettig and Petey. Zymak was very quiet. He felt that he had failed the young man although he had saved his life. We all sat with our drinks and Petey tried to crack a few jokes, but we were bone tired. Anton brought out a bottle, a very strong yellow drink that had little seeds in it, a liqueur, Zymak called it "Polish dynamite." He said the seeds were caraway seeds and that his father and his uncles would drink it after a hunt. Then he talked about his life as a young boy in Poland and about the towns and the noblemen and the castles he had seen. Petey, Rettig and I listened as he talked. He mentioned the Radziwill family and their long history as Polish nobility and their skill as great huntsmen and soldiers. I remember how Rettig's eyes had glistened. Then Casimir turned to me and raised his glass and promised me again that someday, when all this was forgotten, the two of us would go together and stand at the edge of the lake in "Visconsin" and listen to the birds diving and calling to each other in the sunlight.

The Emerald Bracelet

EMILY HAIGHT TAYLOR, a Chicago dowager in her eighties, was found dead last week in her apartment in the Ambassador West. She dined with two friends on Friday evening, two elderly sisters who lived at the Drake Towers. They enjoyed their usual Friday night dinner at the Cape Cod Room, turtle soup with a dollop of sherry, an exquisite filet of sole edged with creamed spinach, a light *Pouilly-Fuisse* with the fish course, and cafe filtre with Italian cookies. It had been their ritual for the past ten years and after dinner Emily always went back to the sisters' apartment for bridge. Later the sisters' chauffeur would drive her in the Bentley to her apartment in the Ambassador West.

By 10:25 p.m. last Friday they finished their game and she was home, sitting up in her bed waiting for Johnny Carson and pinning her hair back when she collapsed. She fell backward on the lace trimmed pillow, gave a little sigh and choked on her tongue just as Carson walked out and Doc Severinson bowed to him with that wiggly, servile gesture. She had been a great Chicago beauty, the daughter of an old banking family, her husband, Dickinson Taylor, dead for twenty years, their children scattered in Aspen, Cambridge and Palm Beach.

Next to the mini-Kleenex box on her night stand was her husband in a mother of pearl framed, gray shadowed Bachrach portrait. The portrait showed a stern faced middle-aged man in a white formal tie, a cutaway and a pince nez.

Hidden in her night table drawer, locked in an old diary, was another photograph. It was a yellowed snapshot of a young man, taken in Paris in 1922 on the Rue Rivoli. He had been her lover, a young Chicagoan with whom she'd had a love affair during the tenth year of her marriage. Her husband had been in Berlin on business. He'd left Emily and the children in Paris for a week alone. She'd met the young man one quiet afternoon with the children at the sailboat pond in the Tuileries. Two nights later he made love to her in his hotel room. He bought her a beautiful emerald bracelet at Cartier's the last afternoon they were together and she'd hidden it all the years her husband was alive. She could have seen the young man again, he also returned to Chicago, but they moved in different circles and they never met. She was filled with guilt and too timid to make an overture to him. He never tried to contact her. Hidden in her drawer was the young, handsome man, shyly looking up into the camera, a tennis sweater tied around his neck. She used the snapshot as a bookmark, locked in the old diary, marking the day he'd given her the bracelet, Valentine's Day, February 14, 1922.

NICK PAPADEMIS worked as a paramedic out of the fire station near the Water Tower on Chicago Avenue. He came to this country from Crete ten years ago. He was a short, good looking man, cocky and unmarried, with a full head of black hair. He wore his hair curled in back and he had a heavy black mustache and dark sad eyes. On the night Emily Taylor died, Nick was the lead in the paramedic squad that answered the call from the Ambassador. The desk clerk had checked Mrs. Taylor's room late that night when she failed to request her customary 8 a.m. wake-up call. When Nick found Emily Taylor, her face was already a pallid blue, her eyes bulging, a fall of gray hair twined on her pillow in a spray of hairpins. He immediately removed her false teeth and dropped them in a plastic drawstring pouch she kept beside her bed. Then he dropped her reading glasses in the pouch and pulled the sheet over her face and with a thick finger touched her eyelids closed. He took off her blue satin scuffs with the coral poufs and placed the slippers neatly under her bed. Nick turned the TV set off, although he stood and watched Rickles for a moment. Then he saw the fragile withered arm dangling from the sheet, with the emerald bracelet hanging loosely, heavily on the thin wrist. He unhooked the bracelet and stuffed it in his pocket.

"Hey, Nickey . . . . ." a man from the squad called from the living room. "Whatta you doing with that old broad? Come on, Nick!" "Come and get her," Nickey Papademis answered. He felt for the bracelet deep in the pockets of his oilskins and carried Emily Taylor, enshrouded in a pink Ambassador sheet, out into the living room.

TATIANA THE BELLY DANCER danced for Nickey Papademis in her bare feet, covering him with her veils and giggling, shaking her long auburn hair at him. Nick was her only customer. It was 4 a.m. Saturday morning at the Hydra, a bouzouki joint on Halsted Street owned by Tatiana's father. Nick had promised himself that he would wait for Tatiana and take her back to his rooming house. Her belly glistened and undulated in front of him. The fragrance of her perfumes hovered over him like incense. He stared at her as she whirled through the smoke, teasing him with her veils and snapping her finger cymbals.

He was drunk. So drunk on ouzo his head kept slipping from his hands to the table. He'd cashed his paycheck at the bar and as she danced he plucked his bills from a water glass where he'd arranged them in an intricate paper fan and stuffed them into her diamond belt. The diamonds of the belt glistened. He was dizzy and he wanted to puke, but he was a fierce Greek warrior and he was too proud to leave the table. He had promised himself to her.

Nick had been dancing all night with the young Greek girls who gathered at the tables of the Hydra like clusters of black sparrows. Now they had gone, drifting quietly away in twos and threes in their black coats and white silk head scarves, and Nickey was alone with Tatiana except for the two old bouzouki players and her father, who was nodding asleep on a stool behind the bar by the cash register.

"What you want from me?" Nickey pulled Tatiana laughing astride his lap, her hair falling over his face. "You want my money, baby? You got my money. You're covered with my money. I got no more." He grinned up at her, showing his even white teeth.

"You got money, Nickey," Tatiana pushed his black curls down on her perfumed breasts. "Tatiana find money." Her hands began working his pockets.

"Hey . . . don't do that, baby!"

"What's this . . . . .?" Tatiana removed the emerald bracelet from the pocket. "My God, Nickey, Nickey . . ." She held the bracelet to the light and the emeralds shone green like the thin eyes of a serpent.

Later, in Nick's rooming house at dawn with Nick asleep on the metal frame bed like a child, Tatiana lit a candle in the cup beneath the icon above his bed, dressed, knelt and crossed herself three times and with the emerald bracelet on her wrist left his room and crossed the street and ran up the church steps to morning mass at St. Gregory's.

GUST KOKINAS, Tatiana's father, was a short, dour looking man with steel spectacles and wisps of thin gray hair on his bald head. His face had almost the texture of parchment in the early Saturday morning light that came through the store front window of the Hydra and shadowed the bar where he and Tatiana sat alone.

When she handed him the bracelet, the old man held the emeralds up to the stream of light and a slow smile froze across his thin lips. "Tatiana, Tatiana, my child. Where you find this?" He wrapped the bracelet over his knuckles and held it to the light again. Then the smile disappeared. "They not real. How I know they real? These gems . . . . you give me fake."

"Emeralds, papa, emeralds. Call Pappas the jeweler. I had it appraised this morning. Emeralds, papa." she said softly.

The old man's bony fingers reached for the telephone.

A T NOON THAT SATURDAY, Gust Kokinas walked up the heavy carpeted stairway leading from the lobby of the Bismarck Hotel to the restaurant on the mezzanine level. He held the handrail as he haltingly ascended the stairs and then stood at the entrance and waited to be seated. He smoothed his hair and followed the captain to a table where a slim, well dressed black man was waiting. The black man was Edward Jeanette, the powerful alderman of Gust's ward. The alderman was alone.

"Are you here to see me about the expressway, Kokinas? I got people coming for lunch. You shouldn't be here. I told you there's no way on the expressway, it misses your property by two hundred feet."

"You can change that, Jeanette." The old man leaned over and spoke quickly. "You can change all that, Jeanette. You make the condemnation take in my property, the restaurant, the building, let the city take it. Everything. Condemn it."

"You want to retire, Gust?" the alderman smiled.

"Sure. Me. Yes. I want to retire." Gust sat back. "I get dizzy now. I want to go to Greece. See my brothers and sisters. An old man. Maybe Tatiana and I stay there."

"Man, you're talking real bread. I mean real bread. Not like that 4 a.m. liquor license. That was peanuts and you don't count so good to start out with."

"Jeanette. You got a wife, no? Maybe a girl? You a man of honor. We trust each other. Here, hold your hand out to mine. We shake hands. Make a deal. Then I leave."

Gust stood up and extended his fragile pale hand to the alderman and pressed the emerald bracelet into Jeanette's palm.

The alderman squinted at the emeralds and then smiled and lowered his hand into his pocket under the tablecloth. He stared at the old man and shook his head. "Whoooooeeee . . . . . Uncle

Gust." The old man just shrugged his shoulders and began to walk away. He looked back once at Jeanette.

EDWARD JEANETTE'S WHITE ELDORADO slid into a no parking zone in front of the criminal courts building at 26th and California. It was 3:30 that Saturday afternoon. A beautiful young black woman in a beige fox fur coat drove. She possessed a model's slim face, high cheekbones, sleek hair pulled back and almond eyes cast like an Oriental. She was Jeanette's mistress, and her brother, a small time drug peddler, had killed a man the week before in a bar on 63rd Street. Jeanette had come to the criminal courts building to see the judge assigned to the case. The state was holding the brother on a murder charge.

Jeanette walked up the stairs into the lobby of the massive gray building and took an elevator to the chambers of Judge Jack Scheinblum.

"I know why you're here, Jeanette." Scheinblum wiped the sleeve of his judicial robe across his mouth. "Your office already called me. It's on that kid that shoved a knife into one of his pals. I got the file right here. They got your boy with three positive I.D.'s. Occurrence witnesses. Clean witnesses, no records. Saw your man arguing at the bar and then he pulls out a knife and shoves it into the guy. The guy fell over dead . . . . it says here, right in the file . . . . his last words." The judge put on his half lens reading glasses and cleared his throat. "'Ritchie . . . why'd you do me like that?'" The judge took his glasses off and sipped his drink again. "It's all wrapped up and ready to go . . . . your man does ten to twenty on a plea, easy. If he goes for broke, he'll get life." Jack Scheinblum shook his beefy head at Jeanette and smiled. "So what you want me to do, Eddie?"

"I hear they got you slated for the Chancery Court."

"Who told you that?" Scheinblum's pale blue eyes blinked.

"The word is out." Jeanette said soothingly.

"Whose word?"

"*The* word, baby. *The* word."

"I should live so long."

"Hey, you're on your way up. Up and out, man. I just come from downtown and I made a *personal* inquiry."

"Yeah, I heard it myself last week. I can't believe it, though. I really can't believe it."

"So relax, Jack . . . . you don't have to come on heavy with me. Three weeks and you're out of here. *Slide* on up to the Civic Center. Take your law books with you, and just shut the door . . . . ." Jeanette made a graceful motion with his wrist. "*Per-man-ent-ly*," he said to the judge.

"Per-man-ent-ly," Scheinblum echoed. The judge's face cracked into a grin. He leaned back in his chair and unzipped the front of his robe and opened another bottle of diet cola from a cooler near his desk and poured a glass for Eddie.

"But you got to come up with ten big ones." Jeanette sipped the drink and laughed. "Ten big ones, baby. Right? As a little contribution to the Party. Ain't that right?"

"So?"

"So you got the bread?"

"Sure I got the bread."

Jeanette smiled again and swirled the ice in the cola drink. "Jack, I know you twenty years, maybe thirty years. You done lots of favors for me. I done a few for you. I know what kind of bread you got and ten big ones are gonna hurt you bad, man. I mean you gonna dig real deep."

"Okay, so it's gonna hurt."

"So maybe it don't hurt so bad," Jeanette said and took the bracelet from his pocket and unraveled it on the judge's desk.

"What the hell is that?"

The judge held the bracelet up like a scuba diver inspecting an exotic underwater creature.

"It's ten grand easy." Jeanette said.

"Where'd you get it Eddie?"

"Don't worry about it."

"They're not hot?"

"Not hot. Very cool."

"You want the boy."

"I want him this weekend, Jack. By tomorrow afternoon."

The judge's big fist shut over the bracelet. "Diamonds don't do me good. I gotta drop that ten grand tomorrow. In the ward committeeman's apartment by four. Whatta I do, Eddie? Hand him a bracelet? He ain't no jeweler."

"It's *arranged,* baby. *Arranged. I have taken care of it,*" Jeanette enunciated each word immaculately. "You just hand the big man the bracelet in an envelope and thank him."

"Arranged?" The judge opened his fist and stared at the emeralds again.

"*Just give him the envelope,*" again the careful enunciation. "I'll take care of the rest. I will . . . . as they say . . . .*convert* it . . . . into cash for the gentleman. Through my office."

"Eddie . . . . ." Scheinblum looked at the alderman again, looked right into his eyes, and then after a moment the judge smiled.

Eddie Jeanette grinned and extended his hand to Scheinblum in an affectionate slap, an athlete's slap, an act of exultation, a ritual among old teammates.

WILLIAM MCGIVERN was a cautious man, equally skeptical in the company of bankers and precinct captains. He was a wary but consummate politician. As ward committeeman, he counted the credits and debits of political favors with the same precision he used to tally the monthly rent receipts from the dozens of buildings in the ward owned by the McGivern Trust. He didn't trust the management firm's computerized summaries. He liked to keep his own figures. His offices were on the second floor of a small bank he established ten years ago on one of his commercial properties. He did his financial business in the bank, but important political affairs, particularly the dispensing of patronage, took place in the living room of his Astor Street co-op on Sunday afternoons. Political patronage was a personal matter to McGivern, and so the old man saved his Sunday afternoons for politics in the muted atmosphere of his luxurious living room, high above the rooftops of his beloved ward where he would sit in his favorite chair with a white silk scarf around his neck, his face occasionally turning toward the windows.

As William McGivern entered the living room, Judge Scheinblum stood up. The old man was dressed in his customary black suit. He walked toward Scheinblum very slowly and extended his hand limply. Scheinblum thought he looked like some ancient priest leading a funeral procession with a lace shawl on his shoulders.

"You're the judge," McGivern said in a weak voice.

"Yes sir."

"Well, I've heard good things about you."

"Thank you, sir."

"Judges are important. The judiciary is important. It has a special function. A noble function." McGivern paused and rubbed his left eye and then a blemish on his cheek. "To be a law giver, to interpret the laws, to judge your fellow men. A great tradition, an opportunity for service."

"I am very humble," Jack Scheinblum said.

"And you're moving up to the Chancery Court, Mr. Scheinberg."

"I am very humble," the judge repeated without correcting the name.

"Mr. Jeanette spoke to me about the matter. A clever man, that Mr. Jeanette. A very good friend of yours, Judge."

"Mr. Jeanette and I have been friends for many years, sir."

"And your friend Mr. Jeanette mentioned you had a unique contribution to make to the Party." The old man smiled wryly at Scheinblum and Scheinblum reached into an inner pocket of his jacket and handed McGivern the envelope. William McGivern took the envelope and nipped it open with a long ivory letter opener. He spread the bracelet out before him on the coffee table. Then seemed to frown, as if the emeralds had suddenly drawn from him a strand of sadness. He slowly picked up the bracelet. Then he shook his head and let the jewels fall through his fingers, inspecting the gems curiously as if each emerald bore an individual message.

Finally, the old man nodded. "I wish you well, Judge Scheinberg," he said, and then his foot reached for a buzzer under the carpet, ringing for a servant. "Pardon me if I don't get up. I wish you good health and many years of service."

EMILY HAIGHT TAYLOR was alone in Parlor B of the funeral home, her coffin flanked by two silver candelabra, the candles flickering, creating moving shadows in the darkness of the room.

It was late Sunday evening. A few friends had called in the afternoon, but since the dinner hour, there had been no more callers. There were only two floral pieces, one from her children and one from her grandchildren. One daughter was flying in from Aspen for the funeral. At 9 p.m. a gentleman arrived at the funeral home and gave an attendant his hat and coat. He then carefully signed the register and entered Parlor B and approached the coffin. He read of the death of Emily Haight Taylor in the Tribune. After dinner at his daughter's apartment he asked his chauffeur to stop for a moment at the funeral home. He told the chauffeur to wait in the car.

The visitor stared at Emily's pale face, and after a moment cautiously touched his hand to her cheek. He slowly knelt down before the coffin and bowed his head and crossed himself. When he arose there were tears in his eyes and he took a handkerchief from his pocket and wiped his eyes and blew his nose. He looked at Emily again and then glanced over his shoulder to make certain he was still alone. She was still beautiful, very beautiful, even in death he thought. The years had been kind to her. He longed to hear her speak to him once more, hear the funny laugh, the deep hypnotic voice he had last heard on a February afternoon in Paris more than fifty years ago. He bent over and lifted her hand, the pale, stiff hand, and held it to his lips and kissed her fingers. Then he put the emerald bracelet back on her wrist and snapped the clasp.

Spring

I T WAS SPRING in 1952 when I stopped going to class at law school. I was a student at the University of Michigan Law School at Ann Arbor, and I think it was spring. There were red flowers, perhaps geraniums, just beginning to come in the Quadrangle. Maybe, though, it was winter. I remember that I had received a postcard from the university inquiring why I wasn't coming to class. I could have written back and told the truth, that I had begun a novel and decided to drop out of law school to work on my novel. Postcards kept coming, though, the last threatening that I would be dropped with failing grades in all my courses. This induced me to temporarily drop the novel and go to the law school and meet my faculty advisor, Professor Marcus Plant, who taught torts.

Professor Plant was a rather earnest young professor. He had a square, open, red face and wore wire-rimmed spectacles. He had a kind of Midwestern openness and frankness combined with a quick intelligence. I would have hired him as my lawyer to represent me against the university, if they were going to sue me, perhaps replevin me back to the law school, but that wasn't their intention.

"Why haven't you been going to class?" he asked when he closed his office door. "You haven't been in class for six weeks."

"I thought I'd quit."

He took my pronouncement with equanimity. "Why don't

you go see someone at the Student Health Service and talk it over?" he told me.

I can't remember if I did go to the Health Service. It was so long ago and the scars of memory have annealed over the wound. I had let down my parents; even though I was paying for law school with my GI Bill tuition, I had let them down. I hadn't told them I dropped out of class. Maybe I'm still lying to myself. I had three years on the GI Bill and I probably used them up before I went to law school, so my father was paying, not me. The tuition wasn't astronomical then, not like today, but still, he wasn't wealthy. He was a salesman, a traveling salesman. He'd never gone to college, let alone law school. I still remember the color of his checks, light green checks with his strong handwriting and signature. They used to arrive like clockwork on the landlady's spindle-legged hall table.

I never finished the novel. I never got beyond three pages. It was about a young man in Ann Arbor who dropped out of the university. The young man is described sitting on the front porch of his rooming house, looking out on the world from behind a veil of hollyhocks. That's as far as I got, the veil of hollyhocks.

In the fall of 1952 I started over again at Northwestern. The only things I took with me were some of the books I had from my year at Michigan: Grismore on Contracts, Waite on Criminal Law, Bigelow on Property. Almost all the professors taught from their own casebooks and they had captive audiences, and of course, captive customers. Even fresh-faced Marcus Plant got into the act with his new casebook on torts, but it hadn't been hardbound yet, so the students bought spiral-bound printed notebooks of Plant's book.

I have some difficulty remembering my professors at Michigan. I will always remember Grover Grismore. He was deathly ill as he stood before us in contracts, his face pinched and drawn by his illness. We were his last class, and I remember the way the clerestory light of the vaulted classroom fell across his gray face as he lectured to us, spectacles glinting from the light, in his worsted suit and vest, a very courageous man.

At Northwestern the books of the Michigan professors were replaced by the books of the Northwestern professors: Havighurst on Contracts, Rahl on Torts, Inbau on Criminal Law, MacChesney on International Law. Even Philip Kurland, newly arrived at the law school, had a red spiral binder on civil procedure. I had already taken portions of some of these courses. I was immediately regarded with awe by my classmates when one afternoon in Havighurst's contracts class I raised my hand and volunteered the theory of third-party beneficiary contractual liability, as if I had invented it. That caused heads to swivel and Professor Havighurst's bony finger to mark my name on the seating chart with his pencil.

Every morning at 8:30 we would begin our day by trudging across the Quadrangle from our dormitory, Abbott Hall, to the law school. Northwestern's law school was another gothic building with gargoyles built like a cathedral but with only one cathedral, and it was smaller than any of Michigan's. We were welcomed most mornings by Professor Daniel Schuyler, who spoke into a microphone about the intricacies of Future Interests. At 8:30 A.M. we would try to keep awake but many of us, having just rolled out of bed and skipped breakfast, fell asleep. I don't think I flashed my legal erudition before Professor Schuyler because, although I had already taken Property I at Michigan, it related only to personal property, and I dropped out after only three or four weeks and never got beyond the Law of Finding. But I did remember the cardinal principle of the Law of Finding was that the Finder had better title to the lost article than any other person in the world except the Owner. So I kept my mouth shut in Future Interests and didn't try to inject the Law of Finding into the Statute of Uses, although I could have done so brilliantly. I was too busy trying to find myself.

Another thing that bothered me at Michigan, other than my unfinished novel and my uncertainty as to the choice of a profession, was a small cyst at the base of my spine. It was congenital but could be removed surgically. It got infected, and I couldn't sit comfortably, so my parents urged me to go into a hospital before I began Northwestern and have the cyst removed. I did, and in a sense I thought the operation would also exorcise the demons that had plagued me at Michigan. However, at the beginning of class in the fall semester, I sat on a small brown rubber inner tube and carried it with me to all my classes. I quickly became known to all my classmates, not only for my precocity but also for my inner tube.

In addition to leaving the hospital with the rubber inner tube, I also left having met several nurses. One in particular, Janet Kurstmann, I thought of constantly. She'd been the nurse assigned to the evening shift and every evening would enter my room at midnight to check on me. I remember the way her starched skirt would rustle and the fragrance of her entrance—there was a certain cologne or hairspray she wore. The first thing I did when I left the hospital was to ask her for dinner.

The nurses at Northwestern Hospital still remain vivid in my mind. There were three of them assigned to my room: Janet—tall, shy, round-faced, sulky, very pretty with her gray eyes and curly brown hair; Connie—short and perky, red hair, tart-tongued; and Mary—tall, thin, also very shy, with auburn hair and bangs. I was the only young man on the floor, and they would each rustle into my room, trailing their respective fragrances, and sponge my face and arms, and take my temperature. I was in a body cast covering my stitches and I was weak, so I was a passive patient. If there was such a thing as a reverse sexual harassment action for unnecessary lingering, brow-wiping, hair-to-cheek touchings, and laughter and teasing, I would have had an extraordinarily strong case. But I never filed it, and instead asked out their ringleader, the night nurse, the sulky Janet Kurstmann.

I had never seen her out of her nurse's uniform. She wore a blue dress that night and looked lovely. I picked her up at the nurses' residence in my father's car, a Buick Roadmaster, shined and waxed for the occasion. This was to be the beginning of a great and enduring love. After all, I had three years to spend at the law school, and she was just down the street in her second year of nursing.

I took her to the Old English Room at the Hotel Pearson. It was a beautiful old room with white tablecloths, heavy old silver, and bone-ribbed framed portraits of English hunting scenes. Janet Kurstmann had silky, long eyelashes and beautiful gray eyes that looked like the eyes of a glazed enamel cat and flashed at me with chinks of fire. How would I ever know that she would soon betray me?

As beautiful and inviting as she was in her blue dress, I blanched when she immediately asked me as the waiter lit the candles, "Do Jews believe in Christ?" I had told her I was Jewish. I felt that this innocent question was the question that would be determinative of our entire relationship, and so I was careful with my answer, and she waited for it with a kind of dark intensity, half given, half restrained.

"You know that Christ himself was a Jew," I answered. I could see her face tighten into perplexity.

"The only Jew I've ever met sold caskets to my father." Her father owned a furniture store combined with a funeral parlor in upper Michigan.

Later in the back seat of the Buick I kissed her once and she immediately fell into a kind of trance. I'd never experienced this before and perhaps never since. All I remember is that I kissed her and she seemed after our first embrace to remain in a trance. Her body had gone limp, she didn't move. She was breathing heavily. I didn't know what to do. I presumed that she was waiting to be made love to by me. I couldn't do it, not only because I was a gentleman, but because I was still in the body cast. It hadn't yet been removed.

A week later she accused me of sexual harassment in gossip with her friends. I don't know why. I think it was because I had done nothing. I had entranced her, but certainly not attacked her. Was there an action for sexual entrancement? She would never go out with me again, so I took out the other two nurses, the short redhead and the tall auburn-haired girl. One shook hands with me at the door of the nurses' residence, and the other offered her cheek. I could tell that I had been impeached by Janet Kurstmann despite my perfect defense.

Of course, some of you may ask what I was doing in the back seat of my father's car. I really can't remember. I do remember that the car had a very obstructive gearshift and that to say goodnight in a body cast one would naturally consider the rear seat. I may have invited her into the back seat, but I swear I had no responsibility for her trance.

So I had immediately in law school developed a reputation as a man who knew women, having set up several of my classmates with members of the nursing class. I was on a roll.

It soon became spring again, the second semester, the spring of 1953. Red flowers were sprouting again, this time in the grimy arcade between the law school and our dormitory. The flowers seemed so bitterly red because one of our classmates had committed suicide late that winter. He lived on my floor and shot himself in his room. I don't think it was because of his law studies. We all knew he was severely depressed. He'd stopped going to classes and we saw only flashes of him each day—pale, distraught. We knew he was very ill, and then suddenly he killed himself. Winter was over, and another spring had come, with its red flowers.

Why had he killed himself? I'll never know. Even today, when I bring up his suicide to my classmates some don't even remember him or that it happened. Life has a way of erasing things we don't want to remember. He was a brilliant student but he was so full of pain he withdrew from all of us and became almost a wraith, a pale figure who wandered the dormitory halls. None of us, including myself, reached out to help him. I remember his angry blue eyes, the slight sneer on his lips, as he would pass us unshaven, in his pajamas, as we all rushed out to our morning classes. And then, suddenly he was dead.

When spring came at last that year of his death, I was finally out of my full body cast and had discarded my inner tube and had survived one semester of grades. One Saturday evening, I invited several of my classmates to a ballroom on the North Side of

Chicago, the Aragon, where we could meet young women and dance away the cares and sadness of winter. I had promised my classmates an evening of frivolity, and seven of us set forth on the El, a Chicago elevated train, to Lawrence Avenue on the North Side to the Aragon Ballroom. We were dressed in our tweed jackets with rep striped ties, and gray flannel trousers. We were ersatz Ivy Leaguers on the El, the flower of Northwestern University Law School out on the town. The story of Janet Kurstmann, the Sleeping Beauty of the Nursing School, and her trance had been so often repeated that I had become known in the School as "The Prince," and various versions of my kiss were retold by my classmates that night, riding the El to the Aragon, typically:

> *Sleeping Beauty (asleep for 100 years) is finally about to be kissed by me:*
> *S.B.: At last my prince, you are here. Kiss me. (laughter)*
> *or*
> *S.B.: My prince, I have waited for you for such a long time. Kiss me. (intense laughter)*
> *or*
> *S.B.: Is it you, my prince?*
> *Me: Yes, it is.*
> *S.B.: Do you have the shoe?*
> *Me: I thought you were Sleeping Beauty.*
> *S.B.: I'm Cinderella, you fool! (maniacal laughter)*

Our fellow passengers on the El looked at us with bewilderment and amazement.

The sign of the Aragon Ballroom was mammoth and blinked at us that April night like a lighted minaret of a Moorish castle, spelling out the name A*R*A*G*O*N majestically, it seemed, from the El platform. It was indeed a magical sight, a bright invitation in the darkness of an ordinary Saturday night. We quickly went down the platform stairs to the ticket office.

We were determined to find frivolity in our springtime away from the law school and the shadow of our dead classmate and when the ticket taker told us that we had arrived on "over 40" night, it didn't deter us. I remember ascending the great staircase, the wafting fragrances that came filtering down from the ballroom, the funereal marble vases and urns in alcoves, and then the sudden darkness of the huge ballroom floor, an artificial sky twinkling above us, and shadowy forms of dancers twirling across the floor, the band far in the distance, in a blue haze.

We moved counterclockwise around the women seated on velvet banquettes and tufted chairs lighted by soft red and violet lamps. The colors and lights were so heavily filtered that no one could really see each other, and so as we asked the women to dance, I'm sure they weren't aware that we were in our early 20's, and we refused to believe that they were all over 40. Anyway, being law students, we were always taught to look for the exception, and as the lights on the dance floor turned blue and then orange and then violet, and Glen Gray and his Orchestra played "Stardust," we danced away into the artificial night.

I, of course, being the progenitor of the evening, would be held responsible for its outcome, but far from being angry, my classmates all seemed to be very happy to have each found an older woman. My roommate seemed the happiest because he never did ascend the mammoth staircase and spent the evening in the lobby with the pale, thin 17-year-old flower girl who was selling flowers from a cart and who looked to me like a student nurse wearing a gardenia.

At the end of the evening some of the frivolity had gone from my classmates' initial assessment and I, being wise enough not to subject myself to more Sleeping Beauty jokes on the El, offered to see my dancemate home. The fact that she lived 6300 South, almost 100 blocks south of the ballroom, one hour each way on the El, didn't dissuade me. My roommate and his new friend, the fragile-faced flower girl, smiled at us as we left. My classmates nodded benignly and smoked their pipes at the cloakroom as they each waited for a woman older than their mother. All of us bought gardenias for our "dates" from the flower girl, and each of us, as a gentleman, escorted our ladies into the soft spring Chicago night.

My friend was a very pretty, red-cheeked, big-busted Irish-American woman of about 45 who had danced and laughed the night away with me, and we became quick friends. I was no longer in my body cast and our age difference really meant nothing to me. I was intent on taking this woman home to her apartment where we would be at last alone and I would overcome the curse of Janet Kurstmann and her league of false-tongued nurses.

We rode the El 100 blocks, holding hands amid all the drunks, me in my Brooks Brothers tweed jacket, she in her black Persian Lamb cape pinned with my gardenia. We were a lovely couple, and Chicago never seemed more magical, until after arriving at 63rd Street when we descended the stairs, I met her policeman brother standing at the bottom. He was waiting to take his sister home. He grunted at me when she introduced us and then I shook hands with her and watched them walk to his car. He was dressed in civilian clothes, had a thick neck and wore an open blue jacket. He looked past me and said nothing. There was nothing to say. I was not the man for his sister, not that night nor any other night. So I shook hands goodnight with her, went back up the stairs and waited for the train that would take me downtown and back to the law school.

When I finally got back to Chicago Avenue, instead of going to my dormitory I walked into the Quadrangle and sat down on a stone bench. It had been a long night. The essence of spring was in this courtyard. Here in the heart of the city there was the odor of damp earth. I could see young buds upon the trees and slips of flowers, always red flowers, heralding new hopes and longings, and also the death of my classmate. So young, such an unnecessary and horrible tragedy in the midst of all our scholarship and energy and all of our desire. Still, it had been nice to dance this night under the false sky, in the Spanish ballroom, moving away from the tragedy of his death, dancing in and out of the lights, feeling the

woman's breasts against me, the light touch of her face, the movement of her eyelashes. It was our shame that he had died and in
some sense, our fault, because we could all sense what was happening and we ignored it. We did nothing about him, carrying on
with law school and our studies as if nothing was happening to
him. We were too foolish, too full of ambition, too angry, too
filled with hope, too full of lies, too self-concerned to acknowledge
death that spring, when everything around us was just beginning
to fill and burst open with life.

Justine

WHEN HE WAS SERVED with the restraining order, he immediately went to see his friend and law school classmate Harvey Wexler of Wexler & Warfield. Harvey Wexler was fit and tan from tennis, and as David told him the story of the Hall of Justice, Harvey snipped at a button on a blue sports jacket with a pair of manicure scissors. He had the jacket spread across his lap.

Harvey picked up his phone. "Alicia, do you sew buttons? Do you have anyone in the pool who does buttons?"

"I don't do buttons, Mr. Wexler, but I'll check, sir."

"I bought this jacket in London a month ago, and the buttons are falling off." He put down the phone. "Now tell me about your Hall of Justice, David. What is it, a Hall of Fame for Lawyers? What's this about a restraining order?"

"I've spent the last three years promoting it, and it's supposed to open this weekend but I've just been enjoined by my partners from opening it. Lawyers and their families from all over the country are coming here to Chicago tomorrow for the opening. It's a building I've developed—a huge glass tower in the shape of the Goddess of Justice, ten stories high, a glass tower. She's blindfolded and holding scales. It's by the expressway in Northbrook. Haven't you seen the construction?"

"I've seen it, but I thought it was a parking garage. It's covered with scaffolds."

There was a buzz, and Harvey answered his phone and switched it on so David could hear.

"None of the secretaries sew, Mr. Wexler, but one of the young lawyers, Linda Whitaker, has volunteered and she'll be in in a moment."

"Do I know her?"

"No, she's only been here two weeks. She's in our litigation department."

"Can she sew a button?"

"She volunteered, Mr. Wexler. I would think it's implicit."

He turned in his seat and folded his suntanned fingers and nodded his head at David Epstein. "A glass tower in the shape of the Goddess of Justice. Are you practicing law or just doing these crazy deals?"

There was a light knock on the door and Linda Whitaker appeared. She seemed to be about 25 and wore a purple tailored suit. She smiled as she looked over Wexler's luxurious office. "I brought my sewing kit, Mr. Wexler. Now where's that button?"

"Linda, while you're sewing, could you look at a restraining order? My client, David Epstein, has been served with this restraining order."

She took a long needle from her sewing kit, and threaded the needle expertly in one motion. She put on her glasses and while she sewed she read the restraining order.

"I don't think they have a case here. They say there's a dispute over your developer's fee. You claim you're due $75,000 as a developer's fee when the project opens. They say you agreed to take an equity position in the project and that you're not entitled to a developer's fee. This kind of suit isn't justiciable in chancery." She wound the button expertly with thread, snipped off the excess, and handed Wexler his jacket. "Where's their irreparable damage? This isn't an emergency, it's just another dispute over money."

"When's the hearing, David?"

"Tomorrow morning at ten."

"I'll get it dismissed, Mr. Wexler. I'll have it dismissed by 10:30."

"Linda, that's terrific. Do you need anything from David other than a retainer check? I think five thousand should cover it."

"I don't have five thousand dollars, Harvey."

"Well, maybe twenty-five hundred."

"I don't even have twenty-five hundred."

"Well, what are we talking about, Dave?"

"We're talking about a free wall space in the Hall of Justice for your firm. You can advertise a panorama showing, say, a meeting of your management committee, with a plaque, WEXLER & WARFIELD, CHICAGO, NEW YORK, LOS ANGELES."

"We also have offices in London, Dubai, Singapore, and Tokyo."

"OK. CHICAGO, NEW YORK, LOS ANGELES, LONDON, DUBAI, SINGAPORE, AND TOKYO. Lawyers from all over the world will see the panorama and bring you business."

"Linda, you go look at it."

ONE HOUR LATER Linda Whitaker and David drove out to the site of the Hall of Justice. As they sped toward it, in his old yellow Alfa Romeo Spyder, they could see the mammoth glass figure of the Goddess of Justice sparkling on the horizon a mile away. It was just as he described it, a colossal lighted glass sculpture of the blindfolded Goddess, holding the scales of justice in one hand and a sword in the other. It glowed blue and slowly revolved over the highway, lighted by spotlights from the ground below which was a kind of park framed with trees and blossoms and a huge reflecting pool reflecting the figure of the Goddess on the water.

"It's just beautiful, Mr. Epstein," Linda said as they drove into the parking lot.

"Please call me David."

"It's just beautiful, David. How does it revolve like that?"

"Actually, it's solar actuated. It catches the rays of the sun and stores them all day, and we use that energy at night to run the solar engine. It's absolutely fuel-efficient and environmentally perfect. Even the glowing blue color, a Chagall blue, comes from the solar energy system."

"And what is she holding—a giant pair of scales?"

"Yes, and they move almost imperceptibly. You can even step out onto them and look out at the horizon or up at the Goddess's eyes, although she's blindfolded. She can't see you, but you can see her."

"She almost looks like the Statue of Liberty, the same tiara."

"She does have the same tiara, but she has her own personality."

"Aura."

"Yes, she does have her own aura."

"Like Aurora, the Goddess of dawn."

"Yes, that's a good analogy."

They stood, looking up at the glass Goddess in the warm, spring moonlight. Just then a guard suddenly appeared. It was Morris, the guard he hired as gatekeeper, a seven-foot man who looked like a gentle talmudic scholar infested with gigantism.

"Morris, it's me, Mr. Epstein, and this is my lawyer, Miss Whitaker. Linda, this is Morris, the gatekeeper of the Hall."

"I'm pleased to meet you ma'am. Things are quiet here tonight, but tomorrow is the opening and there might be vandals. Tonight, just a few old people who want to dangle their feet in the reflecting pool. I told them no dangling. Keep your shoes on. Also some homeless people in cardboard boxes. They've camped out under the folds of her glass toga. I told them no camping under the toga. Tomorrow we're having lots of corporate big shots here, fancy lawyers and their families and clients. This reflecting pool must be kept clean, calm, and serene. We don't want any cardboard shacks under the toga."

"Just as calm and serene as the reflecting pool at the Washington Monument."

"Exactly, Mr. Epstein."

At that moment a dwarf of a man, wizened and bent over,

came down the path. He was dressed in a long woolen overcoat, even in the perfumed spring air.

"You got a cigarette?" he said to David.

"Who's this, Morris?"

"He's my assistant, Samuel, Mr. Epstein."

"Do you really need an assistant?"

"He's the assistant gatekeeper."

Linda smiled at David. "Do you know the story by Kafka of the Hall of Justice and its gatekeepers? The man seeking entry to the Hall of Justice waits forever, and ultimately shrivels up and dies. Samuel and Morris look like they stepped right out of that story."

David pointed to the pedestals of lawyers surrounding the pools. Some of them were empty. "Maybe I should put Kafka up there. I've got Holmes, Cardozo, Brandeis, Thurgood Marshall, Clarence Darrow."

"No women?"

"Well, the Goddess of Justice is a woman."

"Justitia, a Roman goddess. But you should have other women lawyers. Shakespeare's Portia, certainly Anita Hill, Sandra Day O'Connor, Hillary Clinton, Janet Reno ...."

"Do you want to take a skiff over the pool? We're going to offer rides."

Morris held the skiff, and Linda and David got in. Morris acted as the boatman; Samuel, the assistant gatekeeper, pushed them off with his foot.

Morris poled them past a group of old people huddled together in the darkness. The huge boatman shined a flashlight on them. "Please, please, you old people, do not dangle your feet in the pool. Please do not wash your feet in here."

They floated over to the dock, and David held the skiff while Linda jumped off. Morris tipped his hat, handed his flashlight to David, and poled away.

"Here, Linda, there's a moving sidewalk here. I'll switch it on, and we'll take a tour."

"Okay. Could you hold my backpack for a second while I look in my purse for my glasses?"

David examined the pack. "At what age should a lawyer give up a backpack and switch to a briefcase?"

"I don't know, maybe when I'm older. Like 30 or 35. I love my backpack. The other day I was in court and I met my clients dressed in a suit with my backpack They go 'Our lawyer isn't here yet. *He* isn't here.' I go 'I *am* your lawyer. *She* is here.' "

David turned the switch, and they began to move toward the main gate. Samuel, the little assistant gatekeeper in the overcoat that looked like a shroud, suddenly popped up and stopped them.

"Tickets," he wheezed.

"Samuel, why in the world would we need tickets? I'm the owner and developer of this place."

"Everyone needs tickets to everything."

"But we don't have tickets."

"All right—give me a dollar."

"I won't give you a dollar. I am the owner."

"I am the assistant gatekeeper."

"I know you're the assistant gatekeeper."

"We got justice in here. No one gets in without a dollar."

"David, here's a dollar. Give it to him. Stop arguing."

The little old man took the dollar and bowed with a flourish and grinned his gap-toothed grin. "You should have Moses up there on a pedestal Mr. Epstein. He was the first lawgiver. What kind of Hall of Justice is this without Moses?"

They entered a tunnel of darkness on the moving sidewalk that took them to the first panorama, and stopped. There were animated figures of young people behind the glass, like models in a lighted store front.

"What are they doing?" Linda asked. "What's that glop they're putting on their faces?"

"That's a gray cosmetic."

"They look so sallow and gray-faced."

"That's the point of it."

"And the machines spraying their hair?"

"Styling mousse."

"And those pin-striped suits on the rack?"

"Pin stripes for the men, and black suits for the women."

David pushed a button, and the moving sidewalk went up a rise to the next panorama, a window of models of the same lawyers, at their desks in the library of a Wall Street law firm. It's four in the morning; they're asleep at their desks, heads buried in their hands. A catered midnight snack lies uneaten on silver trays on an immaculate white table cloth spread across the top of the bookshelves. A fresh change of clothes for each lawyer hangs in the library closet. The lights of New York blink through the windows. A constant film runs on a screen like a movie in a darkened jet. Films of senior partners on exotic vacations, walking on the Great Wall of China, exploring lamaseries in Tibet, spooning goblets of caviar at the Ritz in Paris, their wives constantly holding silk parasols to avoid the shower of money that follows the partners everywhere, even in cathedrals or museums. There is always a shower of money sprinkling over the partners and their families. The young lawyers sleep at their desks, pin-striped, gray-faced, and hair-glossed.

They stared at the New York panorama, and then David pushed the button again and they moved over another rise. The space was vacant, with a sign "To Let—Your Law Firm's Message Could Be Here," and a phone number.

"Linda, this is the space I could give Wexler & Warfield. We could have photographs of each of your locations, a photo of the London office, Tokyo, photos of all the managing partners. We use wax models made by the same model maker that makes the models for Madame Tussaud's in London." He shined his flashlight on the dark space.

She squinted through her glasses. "Actually, it looks quite nice. And the head of our Executive Committee is named Melvin Waxman. So a wax model of Mr. Waxman would really be cool. And a brass plaque, WEXLER & WARFIELD, CHICAGO, NEW YORK, LOS ANGELES, LONDON, DUBAI, SINGA-

PORE, TOKYO. It would look neat. Mr. Waxman and Mr. Wexler would like it. I think it's definitely a done deal, David."

The next display was a large slate-gray machine that looked like a huge commercial dishwasher or a hospital CAT-scan machine, something you might stick your head in that would send laser beams of X-rays into your brain. It had an opening that was built into the glass display window of the panorama so a viewer could put his head into the machine. The front of the machine glowed with red and blue lights blinking on and off.

"It's a 'Go and Like' remover. It enables you to permanently remove the words 'go' and 'like' from your vocabulary. Also, there's a switch for the removal of 'cool.' "

"It's like so weird!"

"There's another switch for 'weird' and 'freak me out.' For instance, if you want to say 'I go—it's so weird, it like freaks me out,' in describing this machine, you stick your head into it, and those words would be permanently removed from your brain. You could never say them again."

"If I stick my head in there, I'll never, ever say 'go' or 'like' again?"

"Never."

She stood at the machine and hesitated for a moment. "I don't think I'm ready for that."

"Okay. I just wanted to show it to you." He started the people-mover again, and they began to move away from the glowing machine.

"Could I just stick a finger in it?"

"No, you have to put your whole head in it. It operates on the brain."

"You know, David, this is a really strange place, do you know that?"

"It's a strange place, I'll admit that."

He moved them up a floor and they were in a huge, cavernous hall, filled with inflated rubber arms and legs, and neck and body braces hanging from the ceiling. As they moved along the walk, they kept bumping into the dangling inflated arms and legs. They'd bump against them with their foreheads like they were traveling through a sea of inflated beach-toys.

"This is the Hall of Trial Lawyers. I'm sorry, duck your head— I can see that they've hung these inflated limbs too low. Watch it— there's a huge neck brace back there. Just push it aside."

He heard a popping sound and them several more, and a hissing noise. Some of the inflated limbs had popped and deflated. They were hung over an arc of lights and a display of photographs. "These are photos of personal injury lawyers from around the country who contributed to this Hall. It's a Pantheon of Injury Lawyers. Each photo also has a copy of the largest check they've ever received. Some are ten, twenty, fifty million dollars. But the heat from the Pantheon, the lights in the arcade, is rising and causing the displays to pop. I'll have to turn off the lights in the arcade or get smaller bulbs."

They rode over a little bump and were now inside a huge plastic replica of a mouth with gums and several plastic teeth.

"What's this place? It's like we're inside a huge plastic mouth."

"Well, it's the Hall of Dental Malpractice." He shined the flashlight on the tongue and uvula and then on several photographs of lawyers. "We don't have too many contributors. It's a rather arcane specialty."

Again they moved over another small rise up into a tunnel of diffused green light that led to a room of almost complete darkness. The walls of this tunnel were shadowed with green and hung with photos of lawyers that were barely visible in the green murk.

"This is the Hall of Legal Malpractice," David said, probing through the green fog with the flashlight. "It's probably one of the fastest-growing specialties in the country. These are photos of lawyers who contributed to this panorama. I've received more contributions to this hall from the insurance industry than for any other panorama. All the walls in here are papered with money."

"It looks to me like I can just pluck one of those bills right off the wall."

"Don't try."

She put her hand out toward the money, and he grabbed her arm and pulled her hand back just as a school of fish suddenly came snapping at her fingers.

"What in the world was that? Those vicious, ugly fish?"

"The money is only reflected on the surface of the walls, which are really not walls but giant glass tanks filled with client fish. They're more vicious than piranhas. So as you reach for the bills appearing to float on the water, you might lose your fingers or your whole hand to the client fish. I'll have to adjust these safety railings."

He shoved the lever forward and they moved up another rise and suddenly they were in a brightly-lit tunnel. There was the sound of laughter, music, glasses clinking, an orchestra playing.

"This leads to the ballroom and then from here we can walk out onto the scales of justice, if you'd like to see the view." They slowly moved toward the laughter and music and then they entered a huge ballroom with a low, glass ceiling. Couples were dancing, but the women were crouched over. The men were standing up straight, but all the women were stooping with hunched shoulders as they danced. They were all wax figures.

"What's this?" she asked.

"It's an opera. You've heard of *A Masked Ball* by Verdi—well, here you notice all of the men at this ball are also wearing masks. The mask of cordiality, pal masks, mentor masks, sharing masks— and you can see over there a stairway and an escalator. Only men are permitted to go up that stairway. When they do, their masks are abandoned. The women just keep on dancing and dancing alone and twirling hunched over under the glass ceiling."

"Well, I see you can stand here David, but I can't."

"That's true."

"It's grotesque. I'm all hunched over."

"Just keep your head down for a moment and we'll walk over here and step outside and you can straighten up and stand on the scales and get some fresh air."

"No, David. I have acrophobia. I can't go out on the scales. Let's just get out of here. I'm tired of standing in this stooped position."

He moved the lever forward, and they passed through another tunnel that led up to the tower. Linda immediately straightened up. It was very dark, and out of the darkness a light shone in their faces. Samuel was standing there again in his old overcoat with his flashlight.

"Stop! I am the assistant gatekeeper. You cannot come into the tower without making arrangements with me."

"Samuel, it's me, Mr. Epstein. I am the owner."

"I know it's you, Mr. Epstein. I am the assistant gatekeeper."

"I know you're the assistant gatekeeper."

"You cannot go into the tower, Mr. Epstein, without buying an amulet." He opened his tattered coat and there were several charms and amulets pinned to the inside with large safety pins, also several tiny vials in pockets. "For ten dollars I will sell you an amulet that will put you in touch with any lawyer in history. You want to talk to Hammurabi?" He held out a glittering ebony scarab. "I'll put you in touch with Hammurabi. You want Thomas Jefferson?" He held out a whistle. "Blow this, you got Jefferson. You want Abraham Lincoln?" He held a coin bank, a replica of the Lincoln Memorial. "Put a coin in here, you got Honest Abe. Any lawyer you want—I got him. If you want a woman lawyer—I got her. You want to talk to Marilyn Quayle? Shake this bell and you got Marilyn Quayle. Shake two bells and you got Marilyn and Dan—take any lawyer, Mr. Epstein. Take one."

"Okay. Kafka. I want to talk to Franz Kafka."

"For him you drink this potion, and it's fifteen dollars."

"I thought you said ten."

"I said ten, but for Kafka you need a potion, and potions are fifteen."

Linda intervened. She opened her purse. "Here's twenty dollars, Samuel. Don't argue with him, David."

"For twenty dollars you get a choice of two lawyers. I can give you Kafka and also maybe Clark Clifford, or maybe Roy Cohn. Pick one, any lawyer in history."

"Gandhi," David told him. "I pick Mahatma Gandhi."

"Here, drink this. One vial for Kafka, one for Gandhi. For another five dollars you can send them a fax, and they'll be here in one minute."

"Not another dime,"

Linda handed the little gatekeeper a five-dollar bill. "Fax them," she said.

"No, we don't fax direct. First we fax our man at the Wailing Wall in Jerusalem. You leave a message with him, and he will put it in a crevice in the Wailing Wall. He will contact them. Also you can fax a prayer if you want to. Like 'Bless our Hall of Justice.' We will fax back a blessing." Samuel twirled and spat on the ground twice. "We will bless this place and bring you Gandhi and Kafka, but you better do it now, Mr. Epstein. Morris tells me trouble may be coming."

"Here's thirty dollars, Samuel." Linda handed him another five-dollar bill. "Fax Jerusalem, say a blessing, bring Gandhi and Kafka in on the deal. Do anything you have to, but keep this place open one more day so I can go to court in the morning."

Samuel's eyes crinkled, and he took the two vials from his coat and gave each of them to David. "Drink one of these before supper and either Gandhi or Kafka will appear and give you advice. I will fax Jerusalem. A scroll will be prepared. The tower will stand for one more day. I will invoke G-d's blessing. If I can get in touch with Him. If not, I will call Moses, although I haven't seen him for 4,000 years."

"You're 4,000 years old?"

"Give or take a few years. Drink Mr. Epstein. Drink the potion."

David touched a vial to his lips. Samuel put the money in his pouch and jumped aside. The people-mover lurched forward and began slowly up a twisting chamber filled with gray cigar smoke.

Linda and David began to cough and choke in the smoke-filled chamber and then suddenly they broke through the smoke and were up in the tower behind the Goddess's eyes. There was a glass case in the center of the room. Rays of orange light flowed into the room like light flows into the high windows of a cathedral.

"Look at that toga on the model of the Goddess in the glass case," Linda whispered. "It's not exactly something you'd get at The Gap. Look how gray her face is. She looks just like those lawyers we saw with the gray glop on their faces. Are you okay?"

"I feel strange. Very strange."

"What do you mean?"

"I think I see the face of Gandhi down on the reflecting pool."

"Where?"

"Down there. On the surface of the pool. He looks like he's framed with fire."

"I can't see him."

"Can you hear him?"

"No."

"I can. It's almost as if he were up here in the tower with us."

Suddenly the reedy voice of Mahatma Gandhi filled the room. "Ah, Mr. Epstein! Don't worry; the lady cannot hear. Only you have summoned me."

"Yes, Mr. Gandhi. You were a lawyer before you became a visionary."

"Yes, a solo practitioner in Delhi. I had a little office along a canal behind a newspaper shop. I wove cloth there and practiced law."

"And what advice can you give me, sir?"

"Advice—" Gandhi adjusted his spectacles and pulled his white sheet over his thin shoulders. He held his hands before him clasped in prayer. "—my advice is, the white rose has three petals. One is for wisdom, one love, the other is a mantra."

"What is the mantra?"

"The mantra is, 'Never take a postdated check.' You must

chant that to yourself every day you practice law. When I was in Delhi I could paper my office with postdated retainer checks. Only take rupees. Take the cash, and let the credit go."

"Is that it?"

"Omar Khayyam said that and he is indeed older and wiser than I am. 'Ah, take the cash, and let the credit go.' These are pearls of wisdom for the lawyer."

"Is there anything else?"

"One other. If you drink the water of roses, watch out for thorns in the bottom of the bowl. Here you have built a beautiful tower, almost like the Taj Mahal, but you really have nothing here for the people. Not even a fountain in which they can bathe their tired feet. Nothing for poor people. So your tower will fall unless you modify it."

"How to modify it?"

"Ah, that is the question I cannot answer. Only the white rose knows, and that is why it always remains silent."

There was a puff of smoke, and Gandhi vanished.

"Oh my God," Linda said, "I thought I saw the model of the Goddess Justitia get up out of the glass case and leave! There was a puff of smoke and she just got up, put her sandals on, and stretched and left."

"What?"

"While you were talking to Gandhi, there was a puff of smoke and she just opened up the case and left." Linda pointed to the empty glass case. "She's gone. This place is so weird! Samuel, the potion, Gandhi, the sleeping Goddess—" She knocked on the heavy wooden door. "Samuel, let us out of here!"

"Take the parachute," the little old man piped.

"Parachute? David, what's he saying?"

"We have another ride here, a Golden Parachute ride. Corporate lawyers and law professors and their families ride down from the tower on golden parachutes."

David led her out to the parachute ride and strapped them in it, and slowly they descended on two vertical wires with a golden parachute blossoming above them. They could see far out onto the expressways, rivers of cars streaming toward them, the glow of the skyscrapers of the city in the distance. Then they softly hit the ground and were greeted by Morris, the giant gatekeeper.

"They're here burning our law books, Mr. Epstein, the poor people starting bonfires. They keep piling books on and burning them! All our law books. I can't stop them. They're getting ashes in the pool. The poor people—I can't even see them. Also, I think someone threw a brick through one of the panels in the back. I'll show you."

The misshapen giant gatekeeper slowly walked ahead of them with a hand-held speaker. In the shadows of the bonfires he looked like a swollen elephant swaying through the burning grass of a jungle floor.

"Attention, poor people. You must stop burning our law books. We're on to you and have called the police. All you poor people, all you homeless people, the park is closed as of right now. All old people dangling their feet in the pool must stop and leave the premises. All homeless people sleeping here must clear out. The park is now closed. The Hall of Justice is closed. You must leave the premises immediately."

Morris pointed his flashlight at a section of broken glass in the folds of the Goddess's toga that had been smashed by a brick. Someone had scrawled the words "JUSTINE" in whitewashed letters above the tiers of broken glass. There were shards of glass everywhere.

"Vandals," Morris said. "I told you they'd come. I sent Samuel to turn off the engine. We can't let the Goddess revolve anymore. We'll board up the glass, Mr. Epstein. The audience won't see the broken sections if we stop her from revolving. We'll call a board-up service tonight."

"David, if you want to call the police, use my phone." Linda opened her backpack and handed him a portable phone, and he put on his glasses and dialed 911. His head felt like it was filled with burning hummingbirds.

"Hello, police, this is David Epstein of the Hall of Fame of Lawyers on the expressway. We're having trouble here. Vandalism, bricks thrown through glass, people trespassing."

He handed Linda the phone. "They're coming. You don't have to wait. You have to prepare your argument."

"David, there're cabs in front of the hotel over there. I really should go to the office and then to the health club. I'll just jog over and get one. Are you sure you'll be okay?"

Linda looked up at the glass Goddess which had now stopped revolving. The Goddess's face was hidden in a wreath of smoke from the bonfires. "Maybe you should also call the fire department. I'll call them for you. There'll be help here in a minute. Also, don't worry about tomorrow. You'll give your dedication speech and you'll get your check." She shook his hand and began to jog away through the park and he stood and watched her. Just then a drifting blackened page of the Code of Federal Regulations fell on his head like a piece of volcanic ash.

THE NEXT MORNING was beautiful, blue skies, lovely spring weather, sunshine. The Goddess sparkled in the sunlight, and Linda was true to her word. She arrived at the park at 10:45 in a black limousine. He walked through the blossoming apple trees to meet her. She handed him the order permitting the park to open, and a check for $75,000. She also gave him an envelope. "This came for you at the office. Give them a really good speech, David." She got back into the limousine behind the smoked window glass, waved, and in a moment she was gone. He opened the envelope. There was a ticket on a United flight to Los Angeles at 7:00. A note was stapled to the ticket with a name scrawled on it— "Justine."

He walked through the trees past the pool, out of the park, up the stairs to the dais built for the opening ceremony. There were thousands of people waiting in the sunshine. He went up the stairs to the lectern and waved to the crowd. The broken glass in back of the Goddess had been boarded up and covered over with quickly planted shrubs and trees. No one knew about last night's vandalism. He held his hands up to the crowd. There was applause and cheering, balloons floating, and signs dancing in front of him— SOUTH DAKOTA BAR, LOS ANGELES WOMEN'S BAR, YOUNG LAWYERS OF DALLAS—he cleared his throat. WASHINGTON D.C. TAX BAR, PATENT AND TRADE- MARK ASSOCIATION OF BOSTON, COMMERCIAL LAWYERS OF GEORGIA. Off to the side behind a cordon of police in white helmets there was another group holding signs. JUVENILE COURTS ARE CESSPOOLS, NO ACCESS TO JUSTICE FOR THE POOR, INSURANCE COMPANIES OWN THE COURTS, BIG BUSINESS OWNS THE LAW SCHOOLS. A band was playing desultorily. In the front row his partners and their wives sat glaring at him. Their children in Harvard Law and Yale Law sweatshirts were staring at him from their parents' knees. The crowd was spotted with silk parasols of corporate wives, and the noonday sun was bright as the Goddess sparkled in the reflecting pool, and huge fans blew confetti over the audience. He could see Morris and Samuel standing on ladders and feeding bags of confetti into the fans. Behind him the empty golden parachutes were billowing in the wind, moving up and down smoothly on their cables.

"Ladies and gentlemen." He cleared his throat. "Ladies and gentlemen, thank you all for coming. Thank you. This is indeed a very special day for all of us, the opening of a national Hall of Fame for Lawyers, a Hall of Justice. Nowhere else in the country do we have a monument like this, a beautiful tribute to the concept of equality before the law."

"What's in it for the poor?" a loud voice boomed.

There was applause, and a few catcalls.

"On behalf of myself and my partners," he smiled down at them, "I want to announce that all rides on the reflecting pool today will be free, and there will be free flowers for the ladies and fountain pens for the men. For every man a fountain pen, for every lady an azalea, including all the members here of various poor peoples' coalitions. There will be fountain pens and azaleas for everyone. Also, for those of you brave enough to try our parachute ride down from the tower, you will also ride free of charge." There was a cheer from the audience and more applause.

"You can't buy us with fountain pens and azaleas, Epstein," the same loud voice came booming again.

"Also free hot dogs and soft drinks on the first floor at the tent just under the Goddess's toga." This time there were fewer catcalls and hisses.

"For those with a taste for wine there will be two champagne fountains and canapes in another tent. Also free of charge."

The shards of confetti flying over the crowd from the huge fans now became shredded tiny pieces of currency, as Morris and Samuel began to feed bags of currency into the fans. The wives of corporate lawyers automatically lifted their silk parasols, and the Hawaiian delegates released white doves, which flew up and away into the sunlight.

□

THAT EVENING on the United flight to L.A. he watched the destruction of the tower on inflight television. She was smashed by hundreds of poor people, the elderly, the homeless, running through the park in bands, throwing stones and bricks and tossing law books into a huge fire set in the reflecting pool. By 7 P.M. Chicago time the Goddess of Justice had toppled over into her own reflecting pool, a charred, twisted skeleton of glass and aluminum, giving off a cloud of white steam, with a horrible HISS-SS-SS-SS-SS-SS-SS. He'd told his partners to close the park but they wouldn't listen. They were insured. They weren't worried. Anyway, he was fired. He'd given a lousy speech. They were going to sue him and the architect for malpractice. Also, the client fish had bitten two of the partner's wives as they reached for dollar bills, and the wives were going to sue.

The passengers watched the fall of the tower with calm detachment, sipping soda, drinking beer and wine and eating chips and peanuts. Only a baby's crying and hiccups broke the silence. He closed his eyes and turned the earphones to a classical channel and listened to Ravel's "Bolero." He looked out at the vague patterns of the night sky and the traceries of God. He took the $75,000 check from his pocket and looked at it. It was postdated."Men don't cry," he told himself. "Men never cry." So here he was, on his way to L.A., with nothing in his pocket except a postdated check and an overdrawn Visa card. He stared out at the clouds again. There was a face forming in the dark-tinged puffs of clouds. Who was it? The thick dark eyebrows and pale face, the piercing black eyes. The "Bolero" on the headset stopped, and the voice of Kafka came through the earphones.

"You faxed me, Mr. Epstein?"

"Yes. I did. Some time ago."

"The message just came to me. What's your question?"

"Where did I go wrong? You built your tower. It's still standing. Me—my tower fell in a day. My partners and their wives are suing me. I've got a worthless check. Where did I go wrong?"

"First of all, you must realize that there is no Justice. If you think you can build a tower to Justice—forget it—you can't. There is no such thing as Justice."

"So what should I have done?"

"Go to Hollywood and build a tower up in the hills, where they have the HOLLYWOOD sign. Build a tower there, but don't dedicate it to Justice; dedicate it to Condominiums. Condominiums for elderly lawyers."

"Condominiums for elderly lawyers, that's your advice?"

"Yes, condominiums for elderly lawyers."

"What about the poor people?"

"There are no poor people in Beverly Hills."

"I see what you mean."

"Also, hire one of the security services that protects the stars' homes to protect your condominiums. And this time no reflecting pool, David. Maybe a swimming pool surrounded by palm trees, with razor wire in the palm fronds. That's Capitalism. That's Economic Determinism. Forget Justice."

"One other question."

"Yes?" The dark face of Kafka began to fade, and the voice was growing weaker.

"Who is Justine?"

"Justine is Justitia, the Goddess of Justice. She just shortened her name to something Americans can pronounce."

"She was in the glass box. Where did she go?"

"Where did she go? She's a stewardess on your flight. Turn around, David. But stay away from her. Don't pay any attention to her. She's nothing but trouble. You can never please her. She always demands perfection. In seeking Justice and Love we always demand perfection and we always fail."

The clouds dissolved, and Kafka's sad, dark face was gone.

David stared at the beautiful stewardess serving in a blue uniform, a white silk blouse with a white bow, a short skirt. Her hair was tied in back with a black velvet ribbon and a white silver clasp. When she saw him she came over to his seat, looked at him sadly, and touched his hand. Her face was covered with a gray cosmetic and her long, tapered fingernails were painted with gray enamel.

"Go away, Justine," he said. "Leave me alone."

Podhoretz Revisited

H E HAD GONE UNDERGROUND the day after he failed the bar exam. He hadn't thought about it for 30 years, but now, sitting on the flight from Paris to Chicago with the young man beside him studying bar review notes, he closed his eyes and he remembered the pain and how he had immediately gone into hiding.

When the stewardess came around with the wine he nodded pleasantly to the young man. Greenfield held the wine glass up in the beam of his reading light. "À votre sante," he said.

"Santé," the young man answered. "The 'e' is accented."

"I'm sorry, my French is rusty."

The young man didn't smile and returned to his notes.

The kid is really a little shit, Greenfield thought as he looked out the window at the black layers of moonlit clouds. Most of them are insufferable little bastards. They take everything so literally. Had he once been that insufferable? No, he hadn't been that insufferable. He took another sip of the wine.

"Where did you go to law school?" he asked his seatmate with his eyes closed. "I'm a lawyer."

The student, annoyed, put down his yellow marker.

"Stanford."

"My name's Joel Greenfield. I'm a corporate lawyer from Chicago."

"I'm Allan."

"OK—you seem to speak French very well."

"No, I don't speak it well. I hear it well."

"You're studying bar review notes."

The young man began underlining again with his yellow marker and suddenly he stood up, took his knapsack down from the rack, and moved to another seat down the aisle. He turned to Greenfield for a moment. "It's like I don't want to talk," he said, and then slouched down in his new seat.

Greenfield didn't answer him. They were all so goddamned earnest and intense. Had he been that earnest and intense? He'd been loose, casual, graceful, and civilized. He sipped his wine again. He'd known the name of Holden Caulfield's brother, (Allie). No one else in the class knew Allie. No one had even known the name of The Catcher. He also knew that Wallace Stevens, a lawyer, had written "The Idea of Order at Key West," which, gentlemen, more or less explained the universe. It also explained why he hadn't finished two of the questions the first time he'd taken the bar exam and had immediately gone underground for four months.

He looked around the plane and rang the bell for the stewardess. Why not a bottle of Hungarian Tokay and some caviar on those good little crackers Air France served? What was a kid like that doing in First Class anyway? Probably spending more of his parents' money.

He spread the caviar on the cracker and felt the wine beginning to fuzz his mind. It took only about 30 seconds. Everything was absolutely black now out the window. He couldn't tell if he was looking at black clouds or black water.

H E WORE A BLACK COWBOY HAT in 1954. He bought it in Amarillo because he knew he hadn't finished the two questions, hadn't even begun the two questions, so he bought a black cowboy hat and wore it home from Amarillo on the trip his parents had given him. Stephen Schwartz's father had bought him a new car and, after the bar, he and Steve had headed west. First, though, they hit St. Paul because Steve knew a girl there. He hadn't told Steve about the two unanswered questions. So he was alone with his shame in St. Paul and with the girl whose face he couldn't remember now. She was still faceless in his memory but he remembered her shoes. Purple suede shoes with brown saddles. Steve was with the laughing, heavy blonde. He remembered the ornate recreation room. Trying to make it with his date on the narrow floral pillowed rattan couch.

And then Omaha, Denver, and across the mountains into New Mexico. Mexican girls in a tavern in the mountains of New Mexico. The sad high-planed serious face of a beautiful Mexican girl. He hadn't bought the hat yet. He bought the hat in Amarillo. Walking the streets of Amarillo in his gray Brooks pinstripe and wearing the new black cowboy hat. It had a red satin lining and the salesman got up on a rolling ladder to bring down the hat box. It was a shiny black box and when he opened it the red lining flashed up at Greenfield like an open wound. All because of two unanswered questions.

Then over the Ozarks slowly heading back to Chicago, wearing the black hat, lighting candles in tiny mountain churches. Kansas City and the hat. St. Louis and the hat and the pale face of his one true law school love who met him in her driveway wearing an engagement ring. She solemnly asked Greenfield into the house. He could see Steve shooting baskets from the window (she'd turned her face away) and he walked back out to the car without looking back at her and roared out of the driveway, jamming into reverse, leaving a rut in her father's expensive pebbles and never once looking back.

He still hadn't told anyone, not Steve, not the Mexican girl, not his lost love in St. Louis, not anyone.

Then Chicago, his anxious parents waiting at the door with the envelope from the board of examiners. Thick, you passed. Thin, you failed. Alone in the backyard with the thin envelope, still wearing the black hat. Had he cried? He couldn't remember now. It had been so long ago.

H E POURED ANOTHER GLASS of wine and looked out again at
the black patterns of clouds. Had he cried? What difference
did it make? He tried not to look out the window at God's black
patterned handiwork. (What if you fell into one of the crevices,
where would you wind up? What if the plane burst apart and all of
us were cast out like motes adrift in moonlight?) He smiled. He
was good at this. Almost as good as Wallace Stevens. He, Joel
Greenfield, who flew in and out of Paris now like a weary minister.
He, Joel Greenfield, had the same poetic turn as Stevens, even
though his tongue was slightly blurred by the wine, just a tad
blurred. He, Joel Greenfield, who maintained a farm he'd named
Braemor in Barrington with two gun-metal gray Mercedes with
"Braemor" incised in tiny white enameled letters on their front
doors.

Why should a kid's remark set him off?

It wasn't the remark. It was the attitude. "It's like I don't want
to talk." That supercilious attitude.

H E MOVED INTO THE Y on Chicago Avenue and for four
months practiced his timing with an alarm clock. Hour after
hour, working on his timing against the clock like a boxer. Seeing
no one, avoiding his classmates. He disappeared and became a
nonperson. When he surfaced for the next examination he was a
machine. He finished each question with at least four minutes to
spare. As he left the room on the second day, he knew he'd
passed. Six weeks later the thick envelope came and he became a
lawyer. He went to Springfield with his parents for the investiture
and in their album there was still a photograph of him at the base
of the statue of the young Lincoln. Soon after the snapshot, he
entered his law firm, now four floors of the Bank of America
Building, and had simply neglected to mention the failed examination. He said he'd been in Europe at the time of the summer
bar and had returned that February. No one had ever inquired
further.

GREENFIELD DIDN'T SPEAK to the young man again until they landed in Chicago. The law student was cleared to San Francisco and remained seated with his notes on his lap as Greenfield stood in the aisle waiting to exit.

"Allan," he said. "Have you ever heard of Salinger?"

"Who?"

"Salinger. Jerome Salinger?"

"No."

"Do you know Holden Caulfield?"

"Does Caulfield teach at Berkeley?"

"Right."

"I don't know him, but my roommate once went to a conflicts lecture Caulfield gave at Berkeley."

"Good," Greenfield said. "By the way," he touched the young man's yellow-lined notes, "good luck."

In the cab on the way to the office Greenfield thought about why they had called him back again. Jack Podhoretz, the chief tax partner, had died, and he'd been called back from Paris to deal with Jack's widow. They had sealed off Jack Podhoretz's office until Greenfield's arrival. He was the only man in the firm who officially dealt with death. He, Joel Greenfield, was the firm's shredder, the one who went in the office and cleaned it up before the family was admitted. He looked for letters, photographs. Anything the family shouldn't see, he destroyed. He was the only man in the firm who specialized in the cosmetics of death. No matter where Greenfield was—Addis Ababa, Hong Kong, Brussels—wherever a man died the door remained locked until he could fly back and go through the office. He knew where to look for the openings, the cracks, the fissures in a man's character. He could find the hidden stack of ancient love letters, the pornographic photographs, the addresses and phone numbers. He was the firm's Catcher in the Rye. As each of them tumbled over the cliff it was he, Greenfield, who stood waiting to catch them and set them back up again. He arranged their last deceit, healed their last wound, covered their one open fissure. After he had finished, the widow could enter the office and lovingly spend days packing her husband's letters and mementos in cardboard boxes.

He dumped his bags and went down to Jack Podhoretz's office and opened the door. He could smell Jack's pipe tobacco. He sat down at Jack's desk. He had the shredder wheeled in by a gray-jacketed clerk. The man left. À votre santé. À votre santé. He still didn't like to be told how to pronounce his French by a punk kid. If the kid was so smart, let him sit in Jack Podhoretz's chair and figure it all out.

He opened Jack's cabinets. Full of unfiled CCH reports. The letters would be close at hand. Probably shoved under the pile of CCH reports. And there they were. He removed a packet of blue envelopes in a delicate handwriting. They were all from the same woman in Albany, postmarked more than 20 years ago. He read one and then ran them all through. He turned them into blue confetti, blue paper ribbons in a plastic bag. They looked like blue entrails in an oxygen tent. The sound of the shredding was barely audible.

Now a photograph. There would be a photograph of her somewhere. Usually in the right-hand drawer, shoved way in back. If the man was right-handed the photograph would be in the right-hand drawer. He found it immediately. Hidden in an old theater program. She was rather pleasant looking, a bright, expectant, round-faced woman. He looked at her and then ran the photograph through the shredder. There was a slight whirring sound. The kid from Stanford with the yellow marker would some day learn about all this and perhaps be not quite so certain. There would be porno too from the last ten years of Jack's life. You can't be an old tax man without turning into a voyeur. Greenfield sat in Jack's chair and looked around. The letter opener. Of course, the handle of the letter opener. If you stood it on point it cast a shadow on the desk of the figure of a young, pubescent girl, perfectly formed. And the boy? Now where was the boy? The scissors, of course. If you stood the scissors on point, the handle cast a shadow of a tumescent boy. He stood the letter opener and scissors side by side on end and smiled. Oh, Jack Podhoretz, you were a foolish man. Where are you, Jack, a mote somewhere in the universe? Alas, poor Yankele. I saved your ass. He would have to take these playthings away. He put them in his pocket. You see, Allan, the fissures a man falls into, the darknesses, the hidden crevices.

Burak

I RIDE THE COMMUTER TRAIN daily into Chicago to my office on Michigan Avenue, which is the main boulevard of Chicago. Michigan Avenue is lined with beautiful shops and high rise towers and rimmed by a park and Lake Michigan. From my office window I can see the reflection of the Lake and ribbons of traffic on the glass panels of the new building across the street. It's an ivory- panelled tower, a white cylinder built by a Chicago firm and French consortium, it has a beveled roof with wiper blades that clean the glass panels. It looks like a mammoth modern chess piece, a Queen with wiper blades or a giant robot with a beveled forehead.

It's now winter in Chicago. People are bundled up in quilted coats and boots and their breaths leave plumes in the air as I watch them from the train window. Chicago is very gray in winter, but this morning I see a man in a red cap in a scrap yard playing with a dog. I also passed some children in red snowsuits holding hands on their way to school.

I've been reading John Updike's *Bech Is Back*. The main character is a blocked author, Martin Bech, who has recently married a second time after several years of being divorced. He takes his wife to Israel on a honeymoon and in Jerusalem they walk along the Via Dolorosa and also visit the Dome of the Rock where a piece of the peak of Mount Moriah is preserved. Mount Moriah is the mountain from which Muhammad ascended to visit heaven. Their guide pointed to several indentations on the peak and told Bech that the indentations were from the footsteps of the horse Burak on which Muhammad ascended to heaven. I never knew Muhammad rode to visit heaven on a horse, let alone that the horse's name was Burak. It's a piece of information that has been floating in my mind for the last two days and I can't get it out. It's like a loose luminous chip.

Yesterday I told a woman lawyer friend and associate about Burak and she just ignored me. We'd been in the Bankruptcy Court and after losing a contested motion we looked for a place to have a cup of coffee. She and her husband just returned from visiting his parents in Fort Lauderdale. They'd left their young child with his parents and had taken off for the Keys for a few days alone. She was still slightly tanned and hadn't yet acclimated herself to Chicago. So she shivered as she told me that lawyers aren't interested in hearing about Burak. The important thing about a lawyer's life should be "freedom," she said, staring moodily out the window at the bundled figures trudging by in the slush.

"Like in the mornings, Bill really sweats getting to his firm by nine. He just doesn't want to get in after any of the partners. Me, I work for myself, so I don't really care. If I have something to do, I'll get to the office. If I don't, I take my time." She sipped her coffee and stared out the window. "This is a great place, isn't it? You can just sit here hidden and watch people go by. I used to come here between classes at law school."

She is right, of course, a solo practitioner is relatively free. But you're never really free from the pressures of money or the demands of clients; the freedom really is a relative concept. If you're worried about paying your office rent, you're hardly in the mood to debate the relativity of freedom. Also, if you have become tyrannized by irrational clients, you're not on your way to becoming a Philosopher King.

Last night I switched from Updike to Isak Dinesen, the great Danish writer who wrote mostly about her life in Africa. She wrote that birds are really closest to God and unlike people occasionally brush wings with angels. I was at a concert last week at the Public Library across the street. On Wednesdays, they have free concerts, mostly young artists on tour who are passing through Chicago. I heard the pianist Jeremy Menuhin playing Schubert. All through the concert waves of pigeons flew outside against the tall windows. Had I read Dinesen's speculation I would have closely watched the phalanxes of birds for the angels. I didn't see any, but the music and the flights of birds past the windows almost sometime in rhythm were a marvelous mixture. After answering the phone all morning it really calmed me.

I try to spend my lunch hours doing interesting things. Chicago has a great array of ethnic restaurants and shops. Just this week I've already eaten in a Polish restaurant and a Syrian place. After the Polish lunch my friend insisted on taking me across the street where two women were tailoring sheepskin coats in a tiny shop. The women were very shy and barely spoke English. I tried on a beautiful brown suede coat lined with sheepskin with a gray fur collar. I looked like a minister of the Czar right out of Gogol. My friend wanted to buy the coat for me as a gift. It was $300. I've known him for over 50 years, we went to grade school together, and he really meant that he wanted to give me the coat as a gift. I didn't accept his gift. Perhaps I should have. Probably, subconsciously, I was afraid to walk around downtown in such a marvelous strange coat. The shop was full of steam from hissing irons and the women wore men's trousers under their dresses and looked at us sadly when we left empty-handed.

My life as a lawyer isn't all concerts and exotic restaurants. I'm working on this piece today in a cab on the way to a client conference. Crosstown traffic is paralyzed. I have just broken out of the crush of thousands of commuters at Union Station. I was able to break away for a moment for a cup of coffee. I could barely get through the crowd into the cafeteria. People are very angry on the way to work. Mouths set, unsmiling, the workers are much younger than I, in their 20's and 30's. They're all caught up in our obsession with time, work and order. There are clocks everywhere in the station blinking out the time, 8:37, 8:42, 8:39, they all give different times. I look for lawyer friends in the crowd. I see a man I know. He's older now, and bent over from arthritis and walks slowly behind the crowd of young workers. The clock on the face of the Wrigley Building is exactly at 9:00 as I arrive at my office.

I like the way the sunlight in my office touches upon the walls. I have a rather eclectic collection of things in my office. A pyramid of marbles my daughter made, a pencil can made of painted popsicle sticks, a wooden Viking soldier with a gray beard of fluff. I have a stereo and in the late afternoons I often listen to classical music, usually to wind the day down, but often to drown out the angry voice of the lawyer in the office next to me. I have several paintings, one of a bird in flight, a vivid blue painting, an abstract bird. In the morning light the blue is very fresh. I have a fern plant and a tiny portable fan. When I turn the fan on, its breeze comes at me through the softness of the fern. I also have a portrait of our three children and a snapshot of my wife with our dog on her lap. The snapshot of my wife rests against a seashell. I have lots of novels and other books in my bookshelf, but I seldom read them in my office. I have been a lawyer for 37 years. I have my diploma and my license framed on the wall.

When I began as a young lawyer I was sent to a family friend who supposedly might offer me a job. Instead of a job, he gave me some advice: "Save your money, kid." When I took the Bar, the lawyer who addressed us at the induction ceremony gave us this advice: "Nothing is more important than your health." Another friend of my father's gave me a $20 gold piece when I sent out my announcements: "Never spend it," he told me. Within two weeks I had pawned it to pay my office bills.

Now, many years later, I have learned about Burak, that he was a winged horse with a human face and that Muhammad, accompanied by the Angel Gabriel, rode Burak to heaven to visit God and Christ and then returned to Earth. I have also learned that I should not have pawned the $20 gold piece. It wasn't really necessary.

The
Writer's
Chambers

A Woman in Prague

H E SAW HER COMING down the long path between the graves. She was a slim woman with gray hair. When he approached her, he asked her if she spoke English.

"Yes, a little."

"Do you know where the grave of Franz Kafka is?"

She gestured to him to follow. She seemed to be about his own age, in her mid-50s, with once-darker hair streaked by gray. The graves had mostly German-Jewish names, Strauss, Friedlander, Schwarzchild, Weiss. The cemetery was wildly overgrown, and the lanes along the graves were long dirt paths winding under the archway of trees, almost like tunnels edged by foliage and the dark stones.

She pointed. "There, you see it? Dr. Franz Kafka." She nodded and folded her arms.

It was a simple brown granite gravestone with three names, Dr. Franz Kafka, Hermann Kafka and Julie Kafka, in that order. Below it was a newer, flat black marker with faded gold letters, also with three names, Gabriele, Valerie and Ottilie. There were pyres of small stones left on both graves as gifts from visitors, also some coins and a small bouquet of dried flowers. At the foot of the grave, someone had left a plant that now had a single red blossom.

"His youngest sister's name was Julie," he said to the woman.

"No, I believe Julie was the mother."

"I'm sorry, you're right. Ottilie was his youngest sister. The three sisters died in the camps. They're not buried here."

The woman pointed to a marker on the cemetery wall opposite the Kafka grave.

"Yes, I see. Max Brod. He was his good friend."

She sat down on the bench along the wall.

"How long have you been in Prague?" he asked her.

"How long?" She began to count on her fingers. "*Acht* . . . no, in English, eight days; yes, is that right, eight? I am sorry, but my English is not good."

She seemed very sad, she had a thin face etched by sadness. She was dressed in beige slacks with a gray sweater and a brown saddle-leather strap purse.

"You are English?" she asked him.

"No, American. I live in New York and teach at a university there."

"Oh, yes, New York."

"And you?"

"I live in Germany. I teach the children that do not speak." She gestured with her hand to her mouth.

He sat down beside her on the bench.

"Many stones," she said to him.

"Yes, many. Kafka is almost an industry here." He stooped over and found a small white stone and leaned over and dropped it on the row of stones. "There are some coins there too."

"Coins?"

"Yes, people have left coins."

"Oh, I didn't see."

He pointed to the names on the stone. "He is above his father here."

"I don't know if he would like being here with his family. I don't really know." She lit a cigarette.

He thought of the photograph of Kafka and his three sisters, the sisters in immaculate white dresses, all with dark piercing eyes and severe expressions. They didn't look like young people.

"Where do you live in Germany?"

"Live? It is in Heidelberg."

"I live in Manhattan."

"Yes. That is the city."

"No, it is a section of New York."

"English is quite hard for me."

"I speak some French, but you speak English very well."

"No French, please. My French is awful." She grimaced and touched the ashes off her cigarette.

It was very quiet. There was only the muted sound of traffic beyond the walls, nothing else. "We apparently are alone, the only two people here," he said to her after a few moments.

"The only two? I don't understand."

"We, you and I." He pointed to both of them. "At this moment the only two who are with Kafka."

"Oh, I see. Yes. Perhaps. The only two. I think not though." She pointed to the row of stones. "And Brod." She nodded at the marker on the wall.

There were several lines of Czech on Max Brod's memorial. He recognized the word for editor, *redaktor,* and showed it to her.

She turned and he watched her face as she turned, a long, angular face, and dark eyes. She was still a beautiful woman. "Do you speak any Czech?" he asked her.

"No, nothing. A few words."

"Have you always lived in Germany?"

"No. I am from Hungary. I am Hungarian."

"Are you Jewish?"

"Half." She made a slicing movement with her hand and ground her cigarette out. "Half Jewish and half Christian."

"I am Jewish."

SHE NODDED and looked away down the path. An older man in a flat cap and blue workman's clothes was coming on a bicycle. He bobbed his head to them as he passed.

"I think most of the Jews of Prague are buried here, those that didn't die in the camps," he said.

"Probably most. But also in the Old Jewish Cemetery, there are many graves. This is the new one."

"I was in the old cemetery this morning. I've never seen anything like it. Graves from 1400. Rabbi Judah Lowe is buried there. The miracle rabbi who created the Golem to save the Jews of Prague. I put a stone on his grave."

She smiled for the first time and looked up at him. "I put too. I was at the Old Jewish Cemetery, and I also saw—is that right—saw?"

"Yes."

"The grave of Rabbi Lowe. But where was his Golem during the Holocaust? I have not seen one living Jew in Prague, only gravestones."

"I met some Prague Jews this morning, at the synagogue up the street from the Old Cemetery."

"I have been eight days here, and I have not met one living Jew. Only here, now, you, and you are an American."

"I would like to find a bookstore that has some Kafka material," he said. "I was told there are bookstores on Wenceslaus Square. Do you know where Wenceslaus Square is?"

"Yes, I know these stores."

"Would you care to go there? Did you come on the Metro?"

"Yes, I could go with you. Why not?" She put her purse over her shoulder and stood up. They began to walk away, and then suddenly she turned back and called to him. She pointed to several stones on top of Kafka's monument. "You see, one of them is not a stone at all, there it is—how do you call that in English?"

"A snail."

"I have been observing it all the time we have been speaking. Since we first sat down, it has moved from here to here." She traced a line of about six inches.

"Wait for just a moment."

"No," she said. "If you watch them, they won't move at all."

"Where do you think it came from?"

"I think it came down from the trees. On threads, they come

down." She fluttered her fingers.

He looked up at the trees. It would serve him right to meet a woman like this, who knew about snails that descend on silken threads from trees. He would have to come to Prague to find her at Kafka's grave.

"There are raspberries here too," she said.

"And the snails eat the raspberries?"

"No. I ate them. I picked some. They were very good. And the little ones that are crazy for the nuts, what do you call them in English, they also eat raspberries."

"Squirrels."

"Yes, in Italian, *scoiattolli*."

A S THEY WALKED out to the cemetery gate, she pointed to several stones decorated with praying hands.

"Those are the signs of the Levites, the hands at prayer," she told him.

On the Metro, sitting silently beside her, he thought of the suicide of Primo Levi. Levi admired Kafka. He owed it to Levi to come here to Prague to Kafka's grave, and now he had met a woman, a very strange, sad woman, almost as strange and sad as himself. She hadn't told him her name, and he hadn't asked.

At Wenceslaus Square, she took him to a large bookstore and asked to see any books by Kafka in English. She asked in German.

"We have none," the young man in spectacles said.

"None?"

"No, we have no books by Kafka."

"In Deutsch?" she asked.

"No. None."

"No books at all by Kafka?"

He shook his head.

She shrugged, and they walked out, back into the sunlight and the crowds of people in the square.

"We will try another store," she told him.

At the second store, they were taken by a young woman to the manager. "Do you have anything by Kafka in English for the gentleman?" she asked again in German.

"No, madam."

"In Deutsch? In Français?"

"No, madam. None at all."

"In Czechish?"

"No, madam. Not for three years. There is nothing by Kafka in Prague."

"Nothing at all?"

"You will find nothing here."

They left the store and watched some children dancing to rock music in unison in lines under a loudspeaker in front of a record store. They were mostly little blond boys and girls, and they were laughing and doing the steps with their hands on their hips, their eyes bright with excitement.

"Are you surprised?" he said to her and touched her arm.

"I don't believe it. I know one more store. It is over there. I remember it as a literary store. More literary."

A man holding books he was putting up on shelves looked at her without expression. She asked him the same question.

"I am sorry, we have nothing here by Kafka."

"You have nothing at all?"

He shook his head and turned back to the shelf. "He is not available here. No." He bowed slightly with a trace of a smile.

"Ask him if they have anything by Primo Levi."

"No," the man said with the same expression, "we do not have Primo Levi."

"Do you have his brother, Carlo Levi? 'The Christus is Coming to Eboli'?" she said.

"No."

He asked her to join him for dinner, and they went to a tavern and had some Pilsener beer and duck. The tavern was crowded with a busload of German tourists. The men were drinking shots of *slivovitz* and became quite loud. After dinner he suggested to her that they leave and have dessert elsewhere.

It had become dark, and they walked back to the main boulevard and had sherbet in a small café edged by bushes along the sidewalk. She told him a little about herself. She was born in Hungary but had fled the Germans and was saved by the Russians and then went to Italy as a refugee. She was in Venice in the winter. "It was winter," she said, drinking her coffee. "I was 12, I had no money, nothing in the purse. I was what you call an orphan—yes, orphan. We lived in a shack. There was snow on the gondolas. I remember I wanted to taste Coca-Cola. I had heard of it but had never tasted it. To me it represented freedom. So I finally had a Coca-Cola, but it was awful. I hated it. It tasted like poison. Now we have eight McDonald's in Heidelberg and the place for the pizza?"

"Pizza Hut?"

"Yes, a Hut of Pizza has now also come to Heidelberg."

She was staying on the outskirts of the city in a private home. "I told *cedok* that everything they offered was too expensive. I asked them if they had a mission in the train station. They finally found me a private house. I have a room. It is quite far from here."

She asked him no questions about himself. Suddenly, as he paid the bill, she turned to him and asked quietly, "Are you a married man?"

"No, I'm not married. I'm recently divorced."

"I am a married women," she said. She lit another cigarette.

"Where is your husband?"

"He is home in Heidelberg with our daughter."

"You are in Prague alone?"

"One can be quite alone in marriage."

"Yes, and also out of marriage. Kafka, better than anyone, I think, could write about the pain of being alone."

"He was very good with pain," she said. "Perhaps that is why they have banned him here now. Banned, is that right?"

"Yes."

They walked to the Charles Bridge and crossed the old bridge with its ancient statues of saints and the huge castle in the background. There were fishermen below with flat boats in the black water, and white swans on the river. Students were sitting in one of the niches of the bridge and were drinking beer and holding candles, singing quietly to a guitar.

"It would have been very hard for a Jew to hide here," he said to her. "Almost impossible. Everyone is blond. A Jew with dark features couldn't hide."

She stood looking down at the river. "When the Germans came to Hungary, it was late in 1944. We were living in a house. I was a child. The Germans counted 10. Everyone who was 10 had to go. I survived several such counts. But why the Jews went willingly, I do not know. I still do not know. Both of my parents went. I was left alone, only with my cousin. I had in my pocket like this"—she gestured—"a small, how do you call it, nail file." She pretended to hold it in her hand. "I would not let them take me. After my parents went, I swore that if the Germans came to me as a 10, I would do like so." She thrust her hand out. "I would kill whoever came to take me." She turned to him. "You see, I think the Jews felt they had a special bondage with God." She linked her hands. "You know the symbol of Levites? They thought this bondage was special and never could be broken. So the Jews went willingly. God would take care of them." She moved her hands apart and stared at them. "But He didn't." She sighed and shook her head. "I shouldn't talk to you about such things. You are right. It was very difficult to hide. Almost impossible." She turned to him. "It's late. I should go now. You do not have to come to the Metro. We can say good night here."

"No, I want to come with you."

They walked together down along the bridge through the darkness, past the students holding candles, to her Metro stop, where they said goodnight. When he shook her hand, he was surprised at the strength of her hand. It was the hand of a worker, not a woman who taught children. They exchanged cards. After she left, he looked at the card she'd given him under the street light. She had written her name, Nathalia. Her name but not her address.

A Man
in Montreal

HIS WIFE HAD BEEN DEAD for four years. Since her death he'd
had two relationships, both of which collapsed. He'd
stayed away now from women for almost a year. He
seemed not to have the ability to sustain a friendship with a
woman without falling into mourning again for his wife and then,
of course, for himself. It was a paralysis, almost a gray slime, that
gradually had enveloped him and he had lost his capacity to feel
and touch, and had become impotent.

So this week he flew to Montreal for a change of scene and
checked into the Ritz Hotel. His name was Alexander Terraude,
58, an architect from Chicago, with two years of French studies
thirty years ago. He loved Montreal. He'd been there on a commis-
sion for a client last year. He looked French Canadian, with dark
eyes and olive skin, but he was Jewish and not only a Francophile
but also a litterateur and a secret pal of the Canadian novelist from
Montreal, Mordechai Richler, secret in the sense that Richler didn't
know about their friendship.

Tonight about 4, on a Friday evening in February, freshly
shaved and barbered, he was sitting at a table in the Ritz Bar listening to the two women beside him, who were discussing a television
program featuring Dostoevsky's great-grandson. He'd ordered a
glass of Bristol Cream sherry and the waiter in the black jacket had
also brought him a silver tiered tray with finger sandwiches. He
had an identical silver tiered tray to the one brought to the two

women, except his had four sandwiches and theirs had six, and two tiny profiteroles. His did not have a profiterole, but instead had a crenelated paper cup of dry fruit cake. He'd overheard one of the women complaining to the waiter that the tops of the finger sandwiches were stale. "If you keep them wrapped in moist cheesecloth, this wouldn't happen," she said, and then continued on about Dostoevsky. She was an attractive woman in her 60's with a long, thin, finely-boned face, a straight nose, and heavy tortoise-rimmed glasses. She had reddish-gray-blonde curls and was dressed in a blue woolen suit with a patterned silk ascot and gold clip earrings.

After the shampoo and haircut, before coming to the Ritz Bar, he'd taken a short walk around Sherbrooke Street in the slush. They weren't too quick about shoveling the walks in Montreal. They shoveled less and wore boots, but they'd had years of experience in dealing with snow and had just grown accustomed to the piles of heavy gray slush on the walks.

He'd stopped to stare at the window of a condom shop. There weren't any condom shops in Chicago on Michigan Avenue. He could buy the pair of white boxer shorts displayed with pockets and different color condoms sprouting like dead flowers from the rows of pockets. What would he do with a pair of boxer shorts and a pocketful of condoms? What was the child's rhyme, a pocketful of posies, all fall down. Now as he sat at a table in the bar and listened to the two ladies gossiping, he heard one of them say in French, "Au contraire," and tilt her head in mock surprise. He closed his eyes and sipped the smooth Bristol Cream. He could open up not a condom shop in Chicago, but a conundrum shop. He would sell a tonic water, "L'Eau Contraire." What else? He'd seen the word "palimpsest" in the New York Times Travel Section describing the Ritz Bar in Montreal as a "exquisite palimpsest of a bar." Whatever that meant. He could also sell palimpsests in his conundrum shop, but he'd have to look up the word to see what they were. He would sell palimpsests and L'Eau Contraire tonic water. He would also sell boxer shorts with pockets full of palimpsests brightly adorned like posies. If one could adorn boxer shorts with palimpsests. He didn't know, and there wasn't a dictionary within a thousand meters.

"Dostoevsky's grandson," the woman in the blue suit was saying, "Dostoevsky's grandson looked just like an old spaniel." She mimicked the expression. She was very good at mimicry.

"The film was in Baden Baden. They had the grandson there to promote a hotel, the Dostoevsky Hotel, or perhaps a spa. He was a man in his 50's and had that sad Russian face. He seemed so very, very tired." She slumped in her chair. "Maybe it was a new casino in Baden Baden, the Dostoevsky Casino. Or the Hotel Brothers Karamazov. I can't remember which, but the grandson really didn't care, you could tell he was completely indifferent, he just stared at them. They had a translator beside him and apparently the man really was Dostoevsky's great-grandson. He said he was a gambler like his grandfather, that there was a system for roulette that his grandfather had inserted in the novel, 'The Gambler,' and it was actually his grandfather's system and he used the same system. He was such a sad-faced man, with those beautiful, sad, slavic eyes, such a doleful expression." She pulled her face down to demonstrate. "Then the promoters gave him the keys to a car to use for the weekend, a red Ferrari, and can you imagine, he drove it away to see some baron in Liechtenstein who also was a relative of Dostoevsky. He didn't even wave to them. He just took off in the Ferrari and left them all standing there. I was amazed he could drive it." She sat up in her chair and slowly turned the silver tiers of canapes and inspected them and then continued with her story. "Then the film switched to several weeks later, on the outskirts of St. Petersburg. By this time the poor little man somehow had actually purchased a brand new Mercedes. Someone had given him more money for the right to use the Dostoevsky name, so he bought a Mercedes and he was driving it alone to Moscow from Berlin, and he was robbed on the highway near Petersburg. They took the car and all his luggage." She stopped telling the story and sat back and selected one of the finger sandwiches. "Helene, these are so dry I can hardly stand them."

He listened to all this. He had a facility for secretly listening to conversations, like James Joyce, who would sit in the cafes in Paris and listen, and then go back to his room and write it all down. He, Alexander Terraude, wouldn't write any of it down. He would just keep it stored in his head and then later maybe bottle it and put it up for sale in his conundrum shop, "L'Eau de Two Canadian Women at Tea." Or perhaps just "L'Eau de Monreal," without the "T," though. You don't pronounce the T in Montreal.

He was feeling better. He was playing his word games again. An hour ago, before the shampoo and the walk, he was holding a plastic bag the Ritz provided for daily laundry and the perforated strip at the opening of the bag unraveled. It had printed on it, in French and English, that you could use this to tie the plastic bag, and immediately he had a vision of himself in the white tub with the plastic bag over his head, tying the tie around his throat and suffocating himself. It was the way another of his secret pals, the writer Jerzy Kosinski, died, in a tub with a plastic bag tied over his head. Kosinski was a perfectionist. He knew he was losing his physical powers from a debilitating disease, and killed himself before he crumbled in decay. He picked his perfect way, supposedly not painful, a plastic bag over his head in the bath. Even in death, still a Jewish waterchilde hiding in the Polish marshes.

So he, Alexander Terraude, who had lost his ability to make love to a woman, had gotten out of there, out of the room, and shoved the plastic bag and the tie far back on the closet shelf, out of his sightline and out of his reach, and went downstairs for a shampoo and a haircut and then a walk, and then he saw the condom shop and now he was listening to the two women.

The second woman was almost a clone of the first, fair skinned, thin boned, a sharp nose, large glasses dangling on a black ribbon, thin lips, a silk scarf of brown flowers tied around her throat. Both women were in their early 60s. The second woman began to describe a television show she'd seen, a show on Finland and the Tango. "The Finns are very melancholy people. I know this Finnish man in my building, Eino. He's seventy but looks forty, marvelous skin. He's a skier. He's very melancholy and never smiles. I met him on the elevator and said to him, 'Eino, did you see the film on television about Finland?' Everyone is very shy in Finland. The winters are so long, no one smiles in Finland. Everyone is depressed. I didn't tell Eino that. I just told him of the one craze that seems to have engaged the Finns, dancing the Tango.

"Alicia, they've taken up the Tango en masse! Even at lunch hour. Hundreds of people tangoing in these huge halls. But no one ever smiles, not even when they tango together. Also they have lights that flash on and off at the end of each dance, like traffic lights. They'd never ask each other to dance without these signal lights. First the men ask at the signal, the men ask the women to dance, then at the next dance the lights change and the women are permitted to ask.

"I told all this to Eino and he never smiled, not once. All he said was," and here she went into an accent, "'I haff laid two sets of ski tracks this year and already someone hass walked on them and destroyed them. Rather than walk off the trail they walk with their heavy boots in my tracks. I don't think I vill lay a third set.' He hadn't listened to a word I said about the Tango. Only his ski tracks concerned him. That's all he thinks about, skiing."

She reached for a tiny profiterole. "I'd never tango with him, Alicia."

The first woman looked at her and twirled the silver tray. "He'd never ask you, Helene."

They both began laughing.

The bar was filling up now with other women. Two or three sat alone. Women in mink coats right out of one of Richler's Montreal novels, dark faced and exotic. It was one of these dark beauties that he coveted, someone to secretly cover with silks and fragrances. They were selling Patou's "Joy" in the Ritz gift shop. They'd given him a test card and he'd put it into his upper breast pocket. But what could he do with it? Go up to one of these women who'd stopped for a drink after shopping and hand them his scented card of Joy with his room number on it? Hardly. If she'd come to his room, what could he do with her? He could ask her to tango like a depressed Finnish tango-man. Or they could discuss Richler and St. Urbain Street. On the cover of Richler's novel, "St. Urbain's Horseman," there was a rearing horse with its eyes filled with terror. Was that true or did he just dream that there was a horse. He couldn't remember. He'd gone to St. Urbain Street last year, but he couldn't find any Jews; they'd all moved over the mountain, to Outremont or Westmont. St. Urbain was a neighborhood now of Caribbean immigrants. He did find one small frame house, maybe an old shul, that had Stars of David woven into the wooden lattice work of its porch. He'd stood on the porch, alone in the darkness, a hidden Jew from Chicago, tracing the Stars of David in the lattice work with his fingers.

He signed the Ritz check and left the waiter a Canadian dollar, one of their coins, a golden coin. It had an engraving of a loon floating serenely among cattails. The coin was called a "loony," but he was the real loony, an American loony adrift in Canada. He could also sell the golden Canadian dollar coins in his conundrum shop, along with another bottle of tonic water he'd just call "Clair de Lune." One drink and you become a certified loony, floating around and trilling in some dark Canadian forest.

Perhaps he'd go to the opera tonight. Donizetti's "Lucia di Lammermoor." Donizetti went mad like Lucia at the end of his life. Was he going mad?

He left the hotel and walked through the slush. It was maybe minus 30 windchill and he walked five blocks down Sherbrooke to see the Moshe Safdie Museum of Modern Art before he went to the opera. Safdie, an Israel-born architect, had built Habitat on an island in Montreal during the Olympics. Safdie had also built the National Gallery in Ottawa. He wanted to see the Montreal Safdie. So he took himself there in his fur hat and padded coat, looking like any other Montrealer slogging down the boulevard.

At the Museum, he bought a postcard of a Canadian family, a portrait of a family on a Sunday outing, father, mother and daughter, all facing forward, standing in winter in front of each other. They were arranged like a totem pole, each with the same square, gray hat and heavy gray coat and grave expression, the little girl with a white fur muff. He couldn't see the collection because they were closing in ten minutes. As he left, he watched a little French Canadian girl, almost in the identical long coat and muff of the girl on the postcard, staring at her reflection in a glass door. She put her muff down and began to practice genuflecting and crossing herself, watching her reflection in the glass panel. When she saw him watching her, she stopped.

He forced himself to walk the twenty blocks to the opera at the Place des Arts, the Montreal theatre center. When he arrived he was exhausted, but he'd made it, his cheeks glowing, face frozen. He'd forced himself to walk and purge everyone and everything from his mind: Kosinski's suicide, the plastic sack in his room, the two women at the Ritz Bar, even his conundrum shop. The cold, whipping air purged all of it and he felt himself coming alive again and somewhat receptive to what the evening might bring. He bought tickets to Lucia and went into the cafeteria to have dinner. It was about 7 o'clock.

He sat with a salad and a grilled cheese muffin with tomato. He was annoyed that he didn't know how to ask for salad dressing in French, so he ate the lettuce without dressing. He was surrounded by French Canadians and the murmur of French. Mostly single women, out in pairs and threes, laughing, drinking wine, some glancing at him as he sat down. He was lost again in a sea of women, flashing eyes and legs, stripes on stockings, long slit skirts. He cut the muffin into pieces. Why were they all alone? Where were all the French Canadian men? There were a few white-haired men, sitting with their wives and drinking wine. But most of the women were alone. He was an intruder in their garden and later, in the second balcony, he fell asleep while Lucia killed herself. He woke startled and unsure where he was, and joined the applause as the young woman who sang Lucia bowed on one knee, her white dress splattered with fake blood. The women beside him were standing and shouting "Bravo!" He stood and applauded and shook the sleep from his head. Then he followed the crowd from the balcony downstairs and went back into the coffee shop and bought a cup of espresso before he headed back out into the cold.

He sat at a table, across from two women laughing and speaking English and listened to them as he drank his coffee. He didn't want to, but he had to listen. "No sex for twenty-five years." The woman speaking was short, with dark eyes and a round face, maybe Italian or Jewish, and had a quick, manic energy as she smoked and gestured. "No sex for twenty-five years. I don't need it. I've forgotten about it. Lately, though, I take camomile tea and I steam it and take the vapors and have sex dreams. Like a young girl. It's from the vapors. And my skin is so smooth. Like the skin of a baby."

The woman's voice came to him again, as if he had first pushed Pause and now Play. "No, who needs it? I inhale the vapors. Who needs a man? I don't need a man any more. I have a bird instead, a blue budgie bird. Pablito. He likes the dark. He doesn't like it when I take the cover off his cage, so I keep it on when I'm gone. Also, I bought him a companion, a little blue fake bird, and I put her on the ledge in his cage, and he thinks he has a wife. A fake blue lady bird. I let the two of them carry on in there under the cover. Who cares?" She looked directly at him when she said that, as if she'd known he'd been listening to her.

He walked back to the Ritz in the bitter cold. He wound his scarf around his throat in coils, the way the young male students at McGill wore their scarves, coiled around their throats, and he pulled it up over his mouth. It was colder here by far than Chicago, the icicles on the ledges of McGill were almost two stories long, dirty and menacing. On the way to the hotel he noticed an old cathedral and people walking up a set of wooden stairs. He went up the stairs and sat in the cathedral for a few minutes. Mostly elderly people were there. One woman came forward to a statue of Christ and placed her hands on its feet and began praying. When she finished she crossed herself with a touch of holy water and left the cathedral. He sat there and watched the people for another minute, then he left quickly and touched his fingers to the holy water. He stood at the top of the stairs. There was a woman in dark glasses climbing the wooden stairs on her knees. She passed within inches of him, murmuring the name of Jesus, her face contorted with ecstasy. He touched a droplet of snow on her hair as she passed him, still on her knees. She didn't feel his movement toward her, and if she did, she didn't say anything.

When he returned to the hotel he stopped in the Ritz Bar again for a minute and drank a glass of red wine. There were only a few people in the bar. He listened to the piano being played by a man older than himself, a very dignified black man with a white beard stubble. The man at the piano had no expression at all, he was very dour. "The very thought of you"—the man played and sang it slowly, perfectly—"and I forget to do"—lovingly, graciously—"those little ordinary things that everyone ought to do." He repeated the words to himself and sipped the deep, red wine and felt himself growing quiet.

When he went upstairs to the room he broke the plastic seal on the minibar and selected a bottle of Grand Marnier and poured it over ice. Then he drew a bath and emptied a bottle of foam bath into the water. It turned the water blue. He got the plastic bag and tie strip out of the closet and descended into the water.

He slowly tied the bag over his head. It was so gray inside the bag, as if the slime that had enveloped him was now seeping into his head. He took a deep breath and held it. He had the sensation that his dead wife had floated into the bag and she was pressing her lips on his and whispering to him that she loved him. Then she kissed him and floated away. He took another breath and he felt himself growing lightheaded. He tried to say something to his wife to tell her one more time that he loved her. He began slipping back down into the blue water and felt like he wanted to sleep. It was that easy. It would be so comfortable in the water. Then just as he was about to close his eyes he untied the strip and removed the bag from his head. He pulled himself back up in the tub and took deep

breaths, shaking his head and breathing deeply. His eyes were suddenly filled with tiny stars, crystallizing and disappearing like the
snowflakes on the woman's head. He waited for them all to dis-
solve. Then he got out of the tub and, covered with the feathers of
blue suds, put on the terry cloth robe the hotel had provided and
took the plastic laundry bag and the tie strip out into the hall and
tore the strip into pieces and tore the bag in several places so it
would be useless to retrieve it. He left it with the remnant of someone's dinner on the floor on a silver tray with two wine glasses, one
imprinted with dark lipstick. He then went back to the room and
lowered himself again into the scented blue water and closed his
eyes.

That had been too close. He didn't want to die though, he
learned that. He wanted to live. He wanted to live to open his
conundrum shop in Chicago and drink wine and listen to music
and touch a woman's hair and feel her lips on his. He could learn
to love another woman. He would finish the Grand Marnier
before he slept. There was even an electric coil and teapot with
camomile tea among the packets. He would steam himself before
sleeping and inhale the camomile vapors.

Why not, it was worth a try.

Origami
Aeroplane

"I HAD DINNER with Tennessee Williams once," she said. She took a long strand of her hair and coiled it on her finger and then tossed the spiral of hair back over her shoulder. "I was working as an editor for a publishing house in New Orleans and I met Williams. We were doing a collection of his and we all went out one night. I didn't say much of anything to him. Oh, I remember after dinner we were standing in the parking lot, waiting for a taxi, and I said to him, 'The sky looks like a wound.' "

"A womb?"

"No. The sky looks like a wound."

"What did he say?"

"Nothing. He just looked up and smiled."

The man nodded and called the waitress over and ordered his first scotch. The woman ordered a glass of white wine and took a cigarette out and tapped it on the table.

"His brother, Dakin, was also there," she added softly, and then suddenly she was quiet. She had a quick capacity for suddenly becoming quiet.

She must be twenty-four or twenty-five, he thought as he watched her face illuminated by the flare of the match. He was fifty and divorced, with two children. They were in the first-floor bar just off the lobby of the Ritz in Boston. He was a senior editor with a Boston publisher and she'd been sending him chapters of a novel for months. Finally he'd written her a note and invited her to meet him after work for a drink. "The bar of the Ritz at six on Thursday," he'd written on his house stationery. The next day he received a return note from her in a pale blue envelope of the Savoy in London with the address crossed out and her Boston address inserted. "*D'accord*," it said in a tiny, spiked handwriting that resembled his cardiogram squiggle.

The woman had pale ivory skin and long auburn hair. She had a quality of reticence that was extremely appealing to him. She was looking down and away from him now as if she already regretted telling him about the evening with Williams. He wondered if she would get up and leave. He also noticed that she wore a gold serpentine ring and that the eyes of the serpent were green.

She began to speak again. "I knew a man in New Orleans, he called himself an 'old fag' but he was only fifty. Well, this man went home up North to visit his family. He had two weeks and he spent the first week just going to country fairs with his mother and his sisters, eating preserves and pies. I think his sisters were nuns. And then the second week he took off with another man and they came back down and really did New Orleans. The man he brought down with him was a tattooed man and he had only one leg." She stared at him as if she were deciding whether or not she could trust him with this kind of information. "Yes. Well, when they got to New Orleans, the two of them went to their room and they began drinking, and then they decided to streak the hotel lobby. So they did. They streaked the lobby." She smiled and blinked her eyes. She had very dark lashes that she lowered when she decided to be silent again.

"How could a one-legged tattooed man streak a lobby?"

The lashes came up. She looked at him. "He did."

"I believe you."

She nodded.

The man called to the waitress and ordered another scotch and the woman asked for a second glass of wine.

"Have you met other famous writers?" he asked her.

"No. Have you?"

"A few," he said.

He leaned back in his chair and looked around the room. It was done in red velvet but he was feeling rather comfortable with the first scotch gone, almost as if he had climbed inside his cufflink box and the lid was slowly closing over him.

"What did you do last night?" he asked her.

"Oh, I combed the tangles in my cat. I hadn't combed him for two weeks." She looked up again. "Oh, all right, what did *you* do last night?"

"I don't remember. I took my kids to a shopping center for dinner and there were all these little booths. One kid brought back caramel corn, another tacos. I had crepes and asparagus soup. Are you hungry? Have you had any dinner?"

"I'm not really hungry." She paused and drank her wine. "Why don't you order." She lit another cigarette and looked away from him. "Do you think they have a disco here?" She moved her head with the movements of a disco beat and pursed her lips.

"I don't know. Do you disco?"

"I won a championship once when I was visiting a friend at Harvard Law School." She moved her head again and tapped her cigarette. "Disco queen of Langdell Hall."

"You're the Langdell Hall Disco Queen?"

"I think so."

"You aren't sure?"

"No. I'm sure."

"I don't know how to disco," he said. "I like to dance, though. There's music in the dining room. I saw them playing there."

"I don't know how to slow dance," she said.

"You know, you have a quality of diffidence that I like. A quality of cool diffidence. The way you hold your head. The way you hold your cigarette. I see that quality in your writing, too."

"Thank you."

"I like your novel. Why don't we get a room and talk about your writing. You can read from your manuscript."

"I thought you'd never ask." She looked at her watch. "We've been together for five minutes."

"Aren't you into risk? Everyone's into risk."

"A room at the Ritz," she said. "I don't think that's much of a risk. On a scale of risks, I'd say that's quite elegant. Some risks are inelegant, you know."

"I actually knew a man named Elegant," he told her. "I used to swim at a club after work. He was always around the pool and constantly being paged on the loudspeaker. 'Mr. Elegant, Mr. Elegant, telephone call.' I think he was a divorce lawyer and that was a way of advertising." The man was really using up all his material now. That was the lodestone.

"Have you ever heard of the Ritz house detective?" she suddenly asked him. "He's a dwarf and he keeps a cobra in the ventilating shafts." She raised her eyebrows. "He feeds the cobra old rose petals from wedding bouquets."

"What's his name?"

"The cobra's name?"

"Yes."

"I don't know. Charles, perhaps. Charles of the Ritz."

"What's Charles's function? Is he just decorative?"

"Oh, no. He's sort of a thermostat. He pokes his head out of a vent whenever passion rises in a room. He's attracted by any kind of passionate sigh or groan."

"I see. What's the name of the dwarf detective?"

"Wee Willie. Wee Willie of the Ritz."

"What's the name of your cat?" He reached out and touched her hand for the first time.

"My cat? My cat's name is Peter."

"That's a pleasant name. Did you name him after a lover."

She took a deep breath, looked at him, blinked several times, and tapped her cigarette, once, twice, and then she quietly said to him, "I know this Dutch clairvoyant in New York City that I visited last year who told me I was going to marry a tall, blond, balding lawyer from Tennessee and we'd move back down South and I'd begin my doctorate and he'd teach at the law school." He noticed, though, that she was standing as she told him this and she was holding her carryall and her raincoat in her hands. "I know you think I'm laid back," she said, "but I never thought you'd take me literally." She smiled and touched his hand with the finger that bore the serpent ring. "Do you have a reservation for this reading or are you just talking?"

T HEY WALKED THROUGH THE LOBBY and she waited for him by the cigar stand while he went to the desk and asked for a room. When he returned, she was inspecting a box of chocolates with a pink silk bow. He flashed the key hidden in his palm at her and she nodded. They met at the elevator.

"Did you have any trouble?" she asked as the elevator door closed. They were alone.

"No."

"Oh," she said and nodded again. She held her big bag with both of her arms folded around it in front of her. He could see that there were at least two large manuscripts in the bag.

"Do you detect a scent in here?" he asked her and sniffed. "I've heard that they spray the elevators at each Ritz Hotel with the same fragrance."

She sniffed. "I don't smell anything."

"It's true. They spray all of them with a special fragrance."

The doors opened and they went to the room. He hung the DO NOT DISTURB sign on the door-knob. The sign was written in four languages, English, French, German, and Arabic. One of them should do the trick, he thought, and went into the bathroom. He could hear her talking to someone, but when he came out she was alone.

"Who were you talking to?" he asked her. She was sitting in a chair by the window. She'd taken her coat off and put her glasses on and she held a manuscript in her lap. "Wee Willie, the house detective. He was here checking us out."

"The dwarf detective."

She nodded. "He left us this." She pointed to a bottle of champagne in a bucket with two glasses on a table. "This is a nice room, isn't it," she said. She adjusted her glasses and turned on the TV set without sound, using it for light instead of a lamp. She opened her manuscript and began to page through it.

He went into the bathroom again, got a hand towel, and opened the champagne, and poured them each a glass. "What did Willie look like?" he asked her.

"He was very tiny and he had rose petals on his shoulders, also his head was wrapped in a turban with a great big diamond in the center."

"Did he have tattoos?"

"No. He was just a plain little man."

"What did he say? Did he say anything about the cobra?"

"He just said, 'Welcome to the Ritz,' in a tiny squeaky voice, and he asked to see our key." She pulled her legs up underneath her and adjusted her skirt. She also lit another cigarette and began to read aloud to him.

He took his jacket off and then removed his shoes and sat back on the bed with pillows propped against the headboard and watched her. She had a nice reading voice, just a trace of a southern accent. The shadows of the figures on television flickered across her face as she read. He closed his eyes and pretended to be listening with great acuity. Actually, he was thinking about how he could ask her to leave her reading and come to bed with him without really disturbing her. She was like a young butterfly that was only resting for a moment and he was afraid that his least gesture might offend her and she'd flutter out the door. Finally, he decided she couldn't possibly be that fragile and he just asked her, "Why don't you just put the manuscript aside?"

She didn't answer him. She became very quiet and looked at him for a long time and then she tore out a manuscript page and began slowly folding it.

"What are you doing?" He sipped some more champagne. She looked quite beautiful to him in the gray light of the TV.

"You'll see." She kept folding the page and then when she had it folded into a neat little paper glider, she tossed it at him. She tore out a second page and began folding it.

"I hope you have copies of those," he said and sipped the champagne again. He wriggled his toes and tossed the paper glider back at his big toe.

"I think this one is better. Aerodynamically speaking." She walked to the window and raised it.

She stood with her back to him at the open window and then she put her hand out into the darkness. "It's really a soft night," she said.

"Why don't you step back from the window," he asked her gently.

She took a match and lit the tail of the second paper glider and tossed it out the window. "Origami aeroplane," she said to him. She stood watching the flame until it disappeared and then she stepped back and shut the window. Now she came over to him and sat on the edge of the bed and slowly removed her necklaces, and began unpinning her hair. She leaned over him and dropped her necklaces on the night table. As she bent over him, her hair fell loosely around his face. He thought he saw the green eyes of her serpent ring flash at him from beneath the silken umbrella of her hair, or was it a separate pair of hooded eyes staring at him? When she kissed him tentatively, he didn't sigh. He made absolutely no sound. He was beneath her with her back shielding him. If the cobra came hissing out now from the vent attracted by his passion like a heatseeking missile, she would take the lethal sting. He held his breath between tightly compressed lips. He may be sexist, that he knew, even perhaps a sexual adventurist, but it was all part of the literary game and he was an old hand. If there was magic abounding in the room, these were her friends and he knew enough to lie still and be very quiet.

The Pool Party

*"The Pool Party" is a chapter of an unpublished novel, THE
LAST JEWISH SHORTSTOP IN AMERICA. A few months before
publication the publisher cancelled it as being "ethnocentric and
ethnophobic at the same time and besides ... it has no middle."*

*In the novel, David Epstein is a recently divorced real estate pro-
moter who is promoting the construction of a mammoth Star of David
made of glass and containing a Hall of Fame of Jewish sports heroes.
It's solar heated and revolves slowly, glowing Chagall blue and visible
for miles beside the expressway on Chicago's North Shore.*

*Mort Greenberg is David's friend and accountant. Mallory is
David's young teen-age daughter and Blair Halperin is her seductive
friend and the daughter of one of David's principal investors. The story "Justine" grew out of this novel.*

*In this chapter David Epstein helps out at a street carnival in the
suburbs given by friends and neighbors, some of whom are his
investors. The neighborhood children and their parents are the per-
formers. The investors will meet with David after the carnival to discuss the payment of his promoter's fee. He needs the money desperately
to pay alimony and bills and to buy a bookstore he wants to open. The
ten-story-high glass Star of David will be his last promotion.*

H E VOLUNTEERED to be a balloon blower. Mort Greenberg
gave him a tank of compressed air and a bag full of balloons he'd gotten free from McDonald's. He asked him to
make his face up as Ronald McDonald, but he refused. He also
refused to wear Ronald's clown cap or clown outfit that Mort bor-
rowed from the local McDonald's.

"Okay, so be a schmuck and don't dress up for the kids."

"Look, Mort, you want a balloon blower or a fool? You can't have both."

He busied himself with learning how to quickly fill the balloon and tie it off. A line of eager children formed immediately in front of his table.

He kept feeding balloons into fat little hands.

"Mine, mine!" one little girl shouted.

"It's not yours, Charlene, it's mine. He's from McDonald's and he gave it to me."

"Are you Ronald?"

"I'm not Ronald, dear."

"Do you know Ronald?"

"I don't know Ronald." He smiled and handed her a balloon. "Here, Charlene." She didn't take it and the balloon sailed up into the sky. A blue balloon, it sailed above the housetops.

"Ronald, Ronald!" Charlene screamed.

"I'm not Ronald, honey. "I'll give you another, here's a pink one. Hold onto it."

"I want the blue one!" Charlene kept screaming.

"I'm sure Mr. McDonald has another blue one," her mother said. She was dressed in a navy blue Northwestern sweatshirt and white jeans.

"I'm not Mr. McDonald. I'm David Epstein."

"I'm Sandra Nadler. I thought you were from McDonald's."

"No. I live down the block."

"Balloons! Balloons!" some of the three and four year olds were shouting. They were in a line, the little girls holding hands, dark, angelic cherub faces and curls. "More balloons, Ronald," one of them shouted. She giggled and held her hand over her mouth.

He patted her head. "I'm just a daddy," he said and kept filling and handing balloons out as fast as he could. "I'm not Ronald McDonald, I'm just a daddy."

"Yes you are Ronald," the child said.

He saw that Mort Greenberg had left the box with the Ronald

McDonald suit and wig alongside the card table. The little girl pointed to the box. "See? You gots a Ronald suit."

He thought of putting it on. He missed tying at least five more balloons and as he filled them they went sailing over the houses out into infinity. He watched them soaring up, some of them already just tiny colored dots. What would Sandy Halperin and Jeremy Stein think of him if they walked over and saw him in the Ronald McDonald clown suit. Would that be the ultimate obeisance? Would it show them that he was really one of the boys, not some starry eyed elitist? He watched the balloons sail. There was no way he was going to put on the clown suit, not for Mort, not for Sandy, no way, no more self-abasement. He was the only literate man in the town, maybe even in all the suburbs, now that Richard Ellmann was gone from Evanston. Was that hubris? If it was, it was sufficient to keep him out of the Ronald suit.

"Ronald, Ronald!" Charlene Nadler was back, her baby face contorted with rage. "My balloon gone again."

"Where is it?"

"There." She jabbed a finger up. He looked.

"Which one is it?"

"That one."

"The pink one?"

"Yah."

"Okay, here's a green one."

She didn't thank him. She ran back to her mother and threw up her arms and the green balloon soared away. He sighed. Fortunately, he was almost out of balloons.

Mort Greenberg was speaking through a hand held loudspeaker. "Ladies and gentlemen, we're about to start our talent show. If everyone will please step over here, the children are ready now. We've all been waiting for this, our First Annual Talent Show. Ladies and gentlemen, please assemble over here for the talent show. Boys and girls, moms and daddies, grandparents, everyone, brothers and sisters. We have a marvelous show for you, if you'll just come over here."

He put the compressed air tank away in the box with the Ronald suit and folded the card table and chairs and left them in the Halperins' driveway. All the families began congregating in the middle of the block and he walked over and stood behind Blair Halperin.

"I didn't tell Mallory you gave me that blue stone, Mr. Epstein," she said, her eyes narrowing. "Really I didn't. I told her I found it in your driveway and you said I could have it."

"Don't worry about it, honey."

He moved away from her and stood behind the Schendler brothers. They looked like twins, two short, bull necked twins, bald men with bulbous noses in identical striped T-shirts. Were they scowling because they knew what the decision was on his fee? He looked at them. One of them was about to eat a sandwich, holding it on a paper plate.

"Don't eat that, Larry." A harsh voice came from the crowd. A short blonde, presumably a Mrs. Schendler, shouted, "Your triglycerides, Larry." The Schendler brother with the sandwich ignored her and began chewing.

"And now, everyone," Mort Greenberg on the hand held loudspeaker, "let me turn this program over to Miss Melody Stein, the daughter of Jeremy and Lynette Stein. She'll be the program director. Come here, honey. Let's hear it for Melody Stein."

"Thank you, Mr. Greenberg." She was wearing her red Harvard jacket with a Cambridgeiensis seal and she pushed her glasses up on her nose. She had some difficulty holding the program and the microphone at the same time.

Blair Halperin looked at him and shrugged. His daughter, Mallory came over and walked by Blair without speaking to her and settled back in his arms. Mallory stood leaning back on him and he gave the back of her head a kiss.

"Thank you, Mr. Greenberg. Oh, gee. Well, I guess I've got this right. Hello everybody, can you hear?" She tapped the microphone tentatively.

Blair turned and began walking back to her house. He pretended not to watch her as she moved across the lawns. She took her shoes off and went barefoot through some of the lawn sprinklers.

"Okay, I've got it. The program," Melody said. "Let's see. You know, I almost said pogrom, instead of program."

There was a little titter of laughter.

The woman in the Northwestern sweatshirt folded her arms. Her husband next to her was smoking. He noticed that most of the men were cigarette smokers, they were chain smoking even in the relaxed atmosphere of a block party. The men seemed so intense, dressed in pressed jeans and sports shirts with emblems; most of them were younger and none of them was relaxed or acclimated to suburban living. He didn't know any of them. These were city people who six months ago had been living in hi-rise apartments and had spent their childhoods on the West Side or in Skokie. They distrusted suburbia, or at least they distrusted themselves in the country. They were restless, aggressive, urban people and now they were out here in the land of the Wasps with brand new country mailboxes and electric eye garage doors. Most of them were uncertain about the move and this talent show and street fair was really their first group outing.

A scratchy record began playing "You're The One That I Want" as Mort Greenberg nodded alertly to Melody Stein.

"Mr. Greenberg is ready with the music and so we have our very first talent star.

He heard one of the fathers pretending to applaud and saying to the man beside him, "I have to fly to Boston at 6 AM."

"I'm going to New York on the 7:15 flight."

"So what's in New York?"

"A deal."

The first father touched the insignia on his sports shirt. It was an unconscious gesture. "I'm in New York Wednesday."

"Wednesday I'm in LA," the second man said. He picked his frail faced little boy up and put him on his shoulders.

"I'm in LA all day Wednesday, Tucson Thursday."

"Will you be back Friday? I've got Herb Schneiderman and his brother for doubles."

"I already got a game Friday, center court with the pro, eight o'clock."

"I'll see you there, maybe," the first man said.

He glanced across the street at the Halperin house. He saw Blair standing out on a second floor balcony. She looked over the railing and unzipped a beachrobe and wiggled out of it. She was in a white bikini and then she dove over the side of the balcony. He presumed there was a pool below. He didn't know the Halperins had a pool. He hadn't seen one. It happened so quickly. He looked up, there was Blair, and the next moment she dove over the side of the balcony. He couldn't hear a sound of her hitting water.

Melody Stein squinted out at the people before her. "I believe we're about to have a magician." She looked at her list. "Mr. Allen Nadler, and as the magician's assistant, his daughter Charlene Nadler, 4½."

He looked up at the Halperin balcony. Blair was standing there again. She was shaking her head, holding it to one side, try-ing to shake water out of her ear. Then she stood poised ready to dive. She looked like the radiator ornament on a Rolls Royce. She dove over the side and disappeared. He listened for the splash. Nothing.

Allen Nadler began a trick. His daughter Charlene, who had lost both the pink and the green balloons, was dressed as a gypsy and stood in a box with a velvet curtain upon a white garden table. Nadler closed the curtain. "Now, ladies and gentlemen, if you'll please watch the magic box....please give me your attention. A-la-ka-ZAM!" He dropped his magician cape over the box and tapped the box with his wand. He opened the curtains. Charlene was gone.

Allen Nadler was beaming. A tiny girl toddled up to his magi-cian's table and stared at him. She stared at the box and peeked behind the garden table over which Nadler had draped a velvet backdrop. She stared at him again. "Where Charlene?" she asked and the audience laughed. Her grandmother in a yellow T-shirt and holding a white poodle came and took her by the hand. "Charlene gone, Nana," the little girl said.

"Yes, dear, Charlene is gone," Allen Nadler said beaming. He was a Chartered Life Underwriter and enunciated very clearly. He often used magic in his lectures at estate tax symposiums. "Now Charlene's daddy will make her come back," he said with the distinct enunciation. He closed the curtains, twirled once with his cape and unfurled it over the magic box. He tapped the box three times with his wand. When Nadler opened the curtains his daughter wasn't in the box. Nadler looked down at the box and closed the curtain again. His eyes quickly dropped down behind the table, along with his left hand.

He tapped the box again with his wand, three taps, and smiled at the audience. He opened the curtain.

A-LA-KA-ZAM!

Still no Charlene.

There was a murmur of laughter from a few people. Nadler turned his back to the crowd, obviously reaching for Charlene behind the table. His cape was embroidered with gold filigree on red velvet, a swirl of filigree, with embroidered initials forming 2 lines, A. N., C. L. U. He turned his back to the crowd.

"I think Charlene Nadler has disappeared," he said to Melody Stein. "Please call her on the loudspeaker."

The lady beside David nudged him and said, "It's part of his act."

"Charlene Nadler," Melody called into the microphone.

"Where is she, dad?" Mallory asked.

"She's behind the table. Watch, he'll close the curtain one more time and bring her back."

"I have to go now, dad. They're having a baseball game, under lights. An All-Star game. I'm an All-Star."

"You didn't tell me you were an All-Star, sweetheart."

"Ms. Charlene Nadler," Melody called again over the loudspeaker. "Please come back to the magician's table."

He walked with Mallory, one arm around her. "I'm proud of you, babe."

"Come over to the park, dad, if you want, and watch the game. I hope they find Charlene."

"I'll try to, baby, a little later. I've got some business here, so I don't want to promise. If I don't see you at the park, I might be out tomorrow or on the weekend. And don't worry, they'll find Charlene."

She got on her bike with her mitt looped through the handlebars. He leaned to her and gave her a kiss on the forehead. "Hit a homerun for your old man."

"I will, dad." She smiled at him and waved.

"Ladies and gentlemen, please assist us in searching for Charlene Nadler. I'm sure she's right here and she's just hiding. She's playing hide and seek, Charlene, aren't you, Charlene? Come back now. You can come back now, Charlene. Oh, well, I'm sure we'll find her. So while we're looking for her we'll have the next act, Victoria and Matthew Feinberg as Mickey and Minnie Mouse singing the Mouseketeer Song. Victoria is 4 and Matthew is 6 and are the children of Charles and Meredith Feinberg."

Victoria was dressed in a pink tank top with a glittery embossed Minnie Mouse. Her hair was done in a fresh permanent, coils of brown curls. Her brother Matthew wore a blue Mickey Mouse sweatshirt and they both had cardboard oversized mouse shoes and tails that wiggled as they approached the microphone.

Melody Stein bent over and held the microphone for Victoria. The little girl looked at her brother. "M-I-C" she whispered. "K-E-Y" her brother whispered back in her ear and poked her with his elbow.

He walked away and crossed the street to the Halperin house and went around to the back yard. He tried the lock on the gate and saw that it was broken. He walked into the yard where Blair was in the pool doing the backstroke. She was slicing through the water in her white bikini like some Moorean maiden. Blair Halperin was definitely the suburban Jewish version of a Moorean maiden, long brown legs, her blond hair plastered to her cheeks. She should have had an orchid behind her ear and she'd be perfect. She wore a pair of nose plugs and when she saw him standing at the edge of the pool she finished her lap and then pulled herself out and removed the nose plugs and sat at the edge of the pool.

"Hi, Mr. Epstein."

"Hello, Blair. You haven't seen a little girl around here, have you?"

"No, I haven't."

"Charlene Nadler."

"No, I haven't seen her."

"Oh. I just thought that maybe you had."

"Do you want to take a swim? We keep some suits for guests in there." She gestured toward a cabana with two dressing rooms and a built-in hibachi grill.

"No, I don't think so."

"Go ahead. My folks love to have people swim."

"Well, your dad might be looking for me. We still have a business meeting."

"The street fair is so boring. It'll go on for another hour and then there's the baseball game. You should take a swim. It's really nice."

He went into the men's dressing room and held up a pair of flowered trunks. He looked at himself in the full-length mirror. It was either this or a denim suit that was much too small for him. What if any of the Halperins came home and found him in the pool with Blair? So what, was it a crime to take a swim? He'd already played Ronald McDonald and watched Nadler make his daughter disappear. He put on the flowered trunks.

He went out to the pool and she was doing her backstroke flutter kick again. He hitched up the trunks and dove. When he came up to the surface, she was still doing her backstroke. The water really was nice. He floated and did an easy breaststroke.

"Do you want to play some basketball?"

"How can we play basketball?"

"Easy." She climbed out of the pool and went into the dressing room. She came back laughing with a backboard and hoop and a small basketball. She set the backboard up on the deep end of the pool, hanging it over the diving board.

"It's water basketball. Just like regular basketball except you can get out of the pool and dive with the ball."

She tossed the small ball at the basket and missed, and dove back in and he retrieved the ball. He swam back to where he could stand and tried a few shots. Each time she'd retrieve the ball for him.

"Okay, now let's play," she said, swimming to him. "I'll go first."

"I don't know if I'm in shape for this, Blair."

"You're a good basketball player, Mr. Epstein. It's my out." She dove underneath him.

He reached for her and she came up against him. He didn't have the stamina to tread water and here he was with Blair slithering over him. She shot, a long arching shot over his shoulders, and it went in. A bell rang.

"I made it!" He tried to turn away from her and then she swam away from him and climbed out of the pool. He popped out of the water and shook his head. The only sound he heard was a cardinal calling, the distinctive sound of a cardinal calling.

"It's two to nothing," she said, standing above him at the edge of the pool.

"Do you hear a bird?" he said.

"A bird?"

"A cardinal."

"No," she said. She looked down at him and dove.

She came up with the ball.

"All right. It's your shot." She tossed him the ball and he backed away holding it, watching her as she came at him, keeping just her head above water.

"Shoot," she said to him.

He looked at her.

"I'm guarding you, see if you can shoot over me." She extended her arms and then she had her arms around his neck.

"Blair," he said to her.

She was holding on to him like a young gardenia rides on water, fragrant, uncertain, just the two of them in the moonlight.

"Shoot," she said.

Then he looked up and there was someone standing there, watching them. Charlene Nadler in her gypsy girl outfit.

O MY GOD, Charlene Nadler! He had Blair hold the little girl while he went to the dressing room, toweled down and dressed. Jesus, what if they found him in the pool with Blair and Charlene Nadler. He splashed some cologne on his face and pulled his trousers on. He was a menace to the community. He had to laugh, though. He wasn't the menace, Blair Halperin was the menace. He shook his head and brushed his hair and went back out to the pool.

"Gosh, Mr. Epstein, do you have to go?"

Charlene Nadler was watching both of them with her big dark eyes.

"You Mallory's daddy," she said to him.

"Yes." He took her hand.

"Mallory's daddy hug Blair."

"No, Charlene."

"Yah. Mallory's daddy hug Blair in the water."

"No, Charlene, that's bad to say. Charlene should never say that. Charlene should say 'Mallory's daddy found Charlene and hugged her.'" He gave the little girl a hug. "Mallory's daddy found Charlene and kissed her." He gave her a kiss on the cheek. The little girl looked at him with her dark round eyes and pursed her lips.

Blair came back wrapped in a towel. "Here. I want to give you something." She dropped Mallory's blue stone into his hand.

L ADIES AND GENTLEMEN. Mr. David Epstein has found Charlene Nadler. Ladies and Gentlemen——Charlene Nadler!" Melody Stein was beaming. She picked up the little girl and set her on the garden table. Allan Nadler rushed over and hugged her. He shook David's hand. Her mother kissed her and picked her up and carried her triumphantly back to where the grandparents were standing.

"Ladies and Gentlemen, a round of applause for David Epstein. We all thank you, Mr. Epstein." She led the applause and he smiled and shook hands.

"Mr. Epstein." Melody was beside him with the loudspeaker. "Could you just like tell us how you found the little girl?"

"Well, I happened to run into her."

"No, like where did you find her? We looked everywhere."

"I found her at the Halperins. I went over there to retrieve my briefcase. And there she was. She was just standing by the door." He smiled at the people and there was another patter of applause.

Allan Nadler brought Charlene back to the garden table and stood her up. She looked like a veiled Bedouin dwarf in her Gypsy girl outfit.

"Give Mr. Epstein a kiss, honey," Nadler told her. "Give him a nice hug and a kiss."

Melody Stein held the speaker up to Charlene. "Tell everyone, Charlene, where did you go?"

"Charlene's daddy make her go bye-bye."

"And nice Mr. Epstein found you."

"Mr. Epstein hug Blair," the little girl said clearly into the microphone.

"Yes," Melody said, ignoring her. "Your daddy made you go bye-bye and then what happened?"

"Mr. Epstein hug Blair in the water," Charlene Nadler said clearly into the microphone.

THEY WERE BACK in Sandy Halperin's basement. All of them, Mort, Sandy Halperin, Howard Halperin, the two Schendler brothers and Jeremy Stein. No one of course had taken Charlene Nadler seriously. At least he hoped no one had taken Charlene Nadler seriously.

"Okay, Epstein, we've talked this over," Jeremy Stein began. "We've decided to defer your fee for a month or so.

"Defer my fee? What do you mean, defer?"

"We want to get this off the ground before we pay you anything. Howard is willing to fly to Tokyo next week to meet with a Japanese designer. So we'll pay for Howard's trip, then we'll take another look at the whole project and decide about your fee."

"What Japanese designer? Why do we need a Japanese designer?"

"Dave, relax." Mort Greenberg interrupted Jeremy.

"Epstein, I like you," Jeremy Stein continued. "But I don't put my money on people I like. I don't particularly like Howard here. Nothing personal, you understand, Howard. I know you're Sandy's brother. I just don't like all your crazy designs for the Star. But if Howard tells me that's what we gotta do to make this thing go and that we need a Jap designer, then my money rides on Howard. So if I say ten grand gets Howard to Tokyo and back with an expert opinion, why should I throw fifty grand out as front money to you, Epstein, when I don't even know yet if I got a cocoon or a butterfly."

"Jeremy, let me put it in plain English." He tried to keep his voice under control. "This is my idea. The Star of David, the Jewish Sports Hall of Fame. The whole thing. It's my idea. I own it, I have a copyright on it. It's my property. And without my permission, no one does anything. Howard doesn't fly to Japan. He doesn't fly anywhere."

"You have a copyright on the Star?"

"Exactly."

"Epstein, I'm not calling you a liar because I like you, but I don't think you got a copyright on the Star of David."

"Not on the Star of David, Jeremy. On the idea. I own the idea."

"The idea of the Star of David?"

"No, the idea of the Hall of Fame. If you want to build the Star without the Hall of Fame, go right ahead."

"You mean a mammoth Star of David?"

"Right, be my guest."

"Maybe we will. Do you think people will pay to walk around inside it?"

"I don't know, Jeremy. Would you pay to walk inside it?"

"I doubt it. But don't go by me. I don't even go by me."

"Okay, how many mammoth Stars of David are there in the world? What did your daughter say, the Jews have been using it as a symbol since the 16th century. If any Jew in history had been interested in walking around inside a gigantic Star of David, don't you think by this time they would have built one to walk around in? So go ahead and build a Star without the Hall of Fame and see how many paying customers you'll have."

"Dave, don't get hot," Mort Greenberg said.

"I'm not hot. I'm just talking Jeremy's language. I like Jeremy but I don't like his notions of when I should get paid."

"David," Sandy Halperin interrupted, "we don't want this to get complicated. We just thought it important that we get some input from Japan."

"Why input from Japan? I can't understand you guys. Why don't you fly to Israel and get an Israeli architect?"

"David." Sandy took his glasses off and rubbed the bridge of his nose. "Could you please excuse yourself for a moment? Just step outside. I have a notion we could resolve this if you'd give us a minute."

He walked up the stairs and went out the side door and stood in the driveway. The electric garage door was opening and Blair was backing the Mercedes out. She buzzed the driver's window down when she saw him.

"I'm going down to the park to watch Mallory and some of my friends play baseball." She turned her face to him, "I can't stand my hair. Every time I try to comb these bangs down they come back up." She buzzed the window up and backed out of the drive.

"Okay, David, we're ready for you," Sandy Halperin called

through the open garage door. "But just a minute, I want to speak to you privately before we go downstairs."

Sandy Halperin looked around and his left eye twitched. "The little girl in the Gypsy outfit, did you hear what she said?"

"No, I didn't hear her say anything."

"You didn't hear her say, 'Mr. Epstein hug Blair in the water.'"

"Mr. Epstein what?"

Sandy Halperin cleared his throat. "Hug Blair."

"Blair who?"

"My daughter Blair."

"The little girl in the Gypsy outfit said that?"

"She announced it over the microphone."

"No, no, Sandy, I heard her. You're mistaken. I think she said 'Mr. Epstein hug hair.' When I found her I gave her a hug. She was bending over the pool and dunking her long hair in the water. So she said 'Mr. Epstein hug hair in the water.' I wasn't really paying attention, but I think that's what she said."

"Oh."

"The other statement would be ridiculous."

"Yes, it would."

"Well, have you talked it over?"

"Come back downstairs, David. They're waiting for you."

Halperin buzzed the electric garage doors down and the garage machinery whined and clanked, leaving the two men in darkness. They picked their way along the wall to the strip of light underneath the door and then went back down to the basement room.

Jeremy Stein greeted him. "We want to think it over for a week."

"A week, why a week?"

"We got some things we want to look into."

"Like what?"

"Just some things."

"You want to take a week. Take a week. Take a month. I don't care. But while you're looking into things, I'm going to shop the deal. It's a good solid deal and I've got a friend in Michigan who can handle the whole thing."

"Dave," Mort Greenberg said.

"I'm going to shop the deal while you guys look into things. That's not being unfair Mort. That's being smart."

He stood up and walked out of the Halperin house up the street through the block party toward his own home. He could smell the sweet odor of petunias and the moon was low and orange in the sky. He walked for a block and the anger gradually left him. He began to count the number of houses with identical spotted green plastic horses bobbing in kiddie pools in the back yards. He could hear swings rotating on their chains in the soft scented wind, and each of the green spotted horses with its wild bobbing eye glared at him.

The Kisses
of Fabricant

A T THE AGE OF 50, Arthur Fabricant divorced his wife, paid his dues with a sophisticated alimony settlement, paid tuition for his twin sons at an Eastern prep school, and promptly lost himself in a darkly hued garden of luncheon dates with younger women. Six weeks after the divorce, he described himself to his therapist as descending into *un jardin noir*. He felt that he was still in a state of psychic rage over his wife's having left him for a 40-year-old Israeli linguistics professor whom she'd met in her graduate program at the University of Chicago. They were now living in a town house in Jerusalem on the Via Dolorosa.

"I don't know about psychic rage, Arthur. Do you think that's apt?"

"All right, I've fallen into this dark garden, Sydney."

"And what do you think you'll find there?"

"I don't know. Perhaps black tulips, perhaps a younger woman who'll fall in love with me."

"We're not talking black tulips, Arthur, we're talking aging. Why don't you reach out to someone your own age, a mature woman you can have a relationship with? Wouldn't it be far less painful?"

"Sydney, look at your wall tapestry. You know, I've never really looked at it. All those felt Indians being shot at by riflemen. And that huge bird hovering. There's a scroll in the bird's beak. It says

'Peace, Peace for the Cherokee, Oh America.' Are you interested in the Cherokees?"

"Not particularly. I found that in New York last year."

"I wish I had a beautiful bird flying toward me with a message in its beak."

"What would it say?"

"It would probably be blank."

The therapist looked at him.

"You don't want it to say anything, Arthur."

FABRICANT, A SUCCESSFUL ARCHITECT, seemed to have no diffi-culty meeting younger women. He was a cultivated, private man with a wistful sense of humor who wore his hair in a gray scholar's frizz and had money to burn. In reply to a questionnaire from his alumni quarterly, he had described himself as a Francophile, a *littérateur,* a good listener, and a gracious credit-card host. This combination of qualities was sufficient to inure to him a group of winsome young companions, each of whom he'd begun to think of as a separate dark flower. It was into their capricious garden he was descending.

This week, his first luncheon was with a woman in her early 30s, a beautiful vice-president of a large toy company. She was very intense, with brown curls and a pale face, and usually wore velvet jackets and brightly colored, low-cut silk blouses to their lunches. They'd met at a Chinese cooking class where they'd been assigned adjoining woks. She'd just returned to Chicago from Hong Kong after a two-week trip, and when he called to confirm their date he heard a beeping sound in the background.

"What's that?" he asked.

"My mail cart."

"You have a beeping mail cart?"

"Yes, when it tracks past my desk, if it has mail for me it beeps."

He met her at noon in the lobby of a French restaurant. She greeted him gaily with "*Ding hao,*" kissed him on the cheek, and handed him a gift. It was wrapped in ornate tissue printed with a design of a turbaned mandarin being served tea in his bedchamber by a sloe-eyed attendant.

"At least he doesn't have a falcon on his wrist," he said, and thanked her.

After they were seated the waiter brought them white wine and Fabricant unwrapped the gift, a box of fortune cookies. He removed one cookie and held it up. It looked in the candlelight like a shellacked, truncated female torso, but he didn't tell her that. He gently cracked it open.

"I don't have my glasses."

"It says, 'Buy IBM, Arthur Fabricant.' "

He laughed and lifted his glass. "Unfortunately, I've just sold all my IBM. Does it really say 'Arthur Fabricant'?"

"Yes, it really says 'Arthur Fabricant.' "

He opened another cookie and handed her the fortune.

"It says, 'Stop smoking.' "

" 'Arthur Fabricant.' "

"No, it doesn't say 'Arthur Fabricant.' I just made that up. They aren't really personalized. They're just modern messages. I thought you'd laugh at them," she said petulantly and drank down her wine.

He sighed, ordered more wine, some onion soup, and a salad, and put the box and the mandarin tissue into his briefcase. "I wish it had said, 'Stop smoking, Arthur Fabricant.' I need another voice in my life, some impartial, decisive voice." She didn't seem to be listening to him, though, and he could sense that her mood, after only one glass of wine, had already shifted toward sullenness.

Later, when they went through the ritual of a good bye out on the street, she shook his hand and apologized for having drunk so much. He moved to kiss her goodbye, but she turned her face and then suddenly told him that on the outside he pretended he was a 50-ish James Bond but inside he was really crawling with worms. She ran across the intersection while the WALK sign was still blinking. He watched to see if she'd look back at him, but she didn't. Why had she suddenly blurted that out? Because he hadn't extravagantly praised her fortune cookies? Why had he let her say something like that without replying? As he watched her disappear into the crowd, he felt a new pulse fluttering in his stomach, and although he never smoked on the street, he lit a cigarette.

H IS SECOND LUNCHEON was with an editor, 25 and auburn haired. He'd met her at a lecture on contemporary Polish literature at the Newberry Library. He was late and she was slouched at the bottom of the stairwell leading to a Greek restaurant, wearing a long tartan scarf and wooden clogs with green stockings. She was reading a collection of British short stories in the half-light of the stairwell.

"You're late, Arthur," she said and he apologized.

They drank some roditys and she touched his glass and told him she was writing an essay on solipsism in Emily Dickinson and that her lover had left her for three weeks and at this moment was on a plane heading for Hong Kong.

"That's funny, I know someone who's just returned from Hong Kong."

"Everyone is going to Hong Kong. I said goodbye to him yesterday. Or rather I watched him go out the door." She had lovely blue eyes and she shook one side of her hair back and then the other and cocked her head. "Arthur, do you know the last thing he said to me before he left? We'd been arguing for a week. Do you know what he said to me?"

"No."

" 'Incidentally, Linda, you bore me.' That was the last thing he said; not even goodbye." She shook her hair back again. "I don't care. I'm glad he's gone. Maybe his three weeks in Hong Kong will give us space."

After lunch they walked over to Michigan Avenue together. She seemed to slouch either because in her clogs she was taller than he or because she didn't want to be seen by her friends with an older man. In the light, though, despite her slouch, she seemed very beautiful. She wore a tailored black wool coat and it was covered with flecks of lint. She should brush it and I should buy a knapsack, he thought. I could wear it with my tailored overcoat and I'd look much younger. Why do all the young people in Chicago dress as if they were in Aspen? At Michigan Avenue he extended his hand. She ignored it and pulled him to her and kissed him on the lips.

"Linda," he said quietly as she walked away, "I'm sorry I'm so disassociated." He didn't know if she'd heard him in the noise of the traffic.

H E MET THE THIRD WOMAN in the evening for dinner and a poetry reading. She was perhaps 30, tall and slim, with long brown hair and gray eyes. They went to a gallery and listened to a Puerto Rican VISTA worker read his street poems and a middle-aged nun with a lisp reading Gerard Manley Hopkins.

After the readings they walked across the street to a bar. She wore a long silk scarf and he drank a Scotch and held the fringe of her scarf in his fingers and asked her if she'd come back to his apartment with him for another drink.

"It would be much too lonely," she said, the gray eyes staring at him. He didn't demur. When they left the bar and shared a cab, he dropped her at her apartment and tried to kiss her but she turned slightly and he kissed her half on the mouth and half on the cheek. I don't seem to have the rhythm for the seduction of the young, he told himself. I always seem to be moving contrapuntally.

In the morning, he called her. There was no answer. Just as he was leaving his name on the tape, she interrupted and said, "Hi." She seemed cheerful.

"What was that, Beethoven?" he asked, referring to the music that had preceded the beep.

"That's part of a Beethoven bagatelle. I had a hell of a time getting it on there just right."

"Actually, I think that's part of Opus 126," he told her. "Would you like to go to another reading next Thursday at the

Museum of Contemporary Art? They're doing Anna Akhmatova."
He was almost saddened when she accepted.

He ate alone in the evening at a Chinese restaurant across from
his office. He was about to taste a piece of lobster gae kow, which
he held on the tines of a lobster fork while he read the paper, when
suddenly he felt that someone was standing beside him. He looked
sideways and up, and there was the same silk scarf and above it the
same woman. She leaned down and kissed him on the cheek.

"Is that really you?" he asked, putting down his fork and giving the fringe of her long scarf another tug. She blinked and
turned back to her friends. "I think you enjoy doing clandestine
things," she said to him as she turned away. Had she said ". . .
clandestine things, Arthur Fabricant"? No, she'd just said "clandestine things." Anyway, eating lobster gae kow in a public restaurant
alone with your newspaper wasn't very clandestine.

THE FOLLOWING DAY he met a fourth young woman for lunch.
She worked across the street at a bank and he took her to a
place on South Michigan Avenue near the Fine Arts Building. The
restaurant supposedly was a haven for artists and musicians, but
someone had recently installed plastic booths and trellises of yellow
plastic flowers. There was an autographed glossy photograph of
Johnny Carson on the wall that faced their booth. The photograph
gave Fabricant a sense of unease, a feeling of being dispossessed.
But his luncheon date was quite attractive, a blonde with her hair
tied into a loose half-knot. She had a sad smile, tiny earrings, and
flushed cheeks, but actually she was very seductive and he
promised himself that he was going to ask her to go to the Palmer
House after lunch and take a room.

"You know, I think I'm turning orange," she suddenly said to
him.

"What do you mean?"

"Seriously." She turned her palms up. "See how orange they
are."

"They are quite orange."

"What do you think it is?"

"I don't know. Could it be yellow jaundice?"

"No. I think I'm eating too much squash and carrots. Too much vitamin A."

Later, when she hesitated in ordering, holding her hair and twisting it and asking whether this was fried or that was in a cream sauce, the waitress brusquely walked away. "I'll be back when you're ready, honey."

"I think the waitress is suffering from terminal brusqueness," he said.

The young woman nodded and sucked in her cheeks.

He asked her to go along with him to the Fine Arts Building and they took the elevator up to the sixth floor. He had no reason to pick the sixth floor but he'd always wanted to just pick a floor and secretly stand in the corridor outside the rehearsal rooms and listen to the music. He never had the nerve to walk past the elevator starter, but today, with the young woman, it seemed very natural. He was certain that they looked like a professor and student. He nodded at the starter and the man shut the ancient cage and smiled, and Fabricant tipped his hat as he pressed the button.

The elevator began to creak slowly upward. When they reached six it lurched to a stop and he pulled the gates open and she preceded him out into the corridor.

They stopped before an office door and listened to a violin. Everything was shadowed and dimly lit. The door was lettered MARIA SCHWARZKOPF—VIOLIN. Fabricant smiled at the sweet music. His companion smiled back at him. "It is beautiful," she whispered. He took her arm.

Each door was filigreed with ornamental beading around the wooden archways.

"I wonder if Louis Sullivan did this building," he said to her. "The work is so intricate."

She held her fingers up to her lips. They were standing before a door marked in thin black letters FREDERICK KUNZ—CELLIST. Her eyes were sparkling.

He watched her and listened to the cello and touched her hair. Now would be the time to ask her to the Palmer House, extend the lunch hour, a few minutes of love, two friends adrift in the city, creating their own island, a sanctuary. He leaned toward her. She moved away from him.

"Do I look orange in this light?" she asked, tilting her face and stopping before a door lettered ANNA T. BOFFO—VOICE.

"No, you look lovely."

She kissed him on the cheek.

"I wonder where 'Anna T. Boffo—Voice' is today," she said, pointing. The pane of glass was dark. "You know, I have an idea for a terrific cartoon." She drew an imaginary line through the word "Voice" on the glass panel. "Anna T. Boffo—Sore Throat," she said.

He sat down at the top of the stairwell and watched her move away down the corridor. She looked like a young nun rustling along a highly varnished corridor of chancery offices.

She returned to where he was sitting. "Don't you think 'Anna T. Boffo—Sore Throat' is a good idea for a cartoon, Arthur?"

"Would you like to go the Palmer House and take a room for the afternoon?"

"Don't you think that's a funny line, Arthur?"

Even with Maria Schwarzkopf and Frederick Kunz playing for him now in unconscious harmony, he knew that she'd never go with him and he wasn't going to ask her again.

"I think that 'Anna T. Boffo—Sore Throat' is funny," he said.

A T THE END OF THE WEEK he asked one more young woman to dinner. She worked at a gallery in Hyde Park that had hung some of his blueprints in a show of architectural drawings. He met her after work and walked her home with her bicycle. He was surprised that she had another bicycle in her apartment, a man's bicycle.

"It belongs to a friend. I should take it back to him, but he lives on the North Side and I'll have to ride it up along the lakefront and I keep putting it off. Would you like to follow me and then go see Fellini's *City of Women*?" She had long black hair and she must be about 24, he thought, as he squeezed the handles of her friend's bicycle. She was actually suggesting a ten-mile ride.

"No, couldn't we just go somewhere around here for dinner?"

She gave him a glass of white wine and some Brie on crackers and took an Irish flute from a small case. She began to play for him. With her cheeks puffed out, she looked like a beautiful young adder and she played quite expertly.

They went to a Chinese restaurant on Dorchester for dinner, and when they returned to her apartment she lit candles, put on a tape of the Irish flute music, and gave him more wine. He tentatively put one arm around her in the kitchen as she poured.

She moved away to the couch in the living room and apologized because some cotton stuffing was seeping from a rent. He sat down beside her. Her hair seemed like black silk in the candlelight. He kissed her gently and held her for a moment and then whispered to her in French.

"*Votre yeux sont bleu.*"

"My eye is blue?"

"Is that what I said?"

"Yes," she laughed.

He plucked at a bit of stuffing, a piece of cotton in her hair.

"I don't think you're really willing to make an emotional investment in me, Arthur," she said, staring at him.

"An emotional investment? What do you mean?"

"I'm very cautious," she told him. "I'm not like the other women you must meet. I'm always very cautious. I have someone who is willing to make an emotional investment in me, so I'm extremely cautious about anyone else, although I'm not really satisfied with the relationship I have," She looked at the bicycle.

"I would be willing to make an emotional investment in you," he told her as she led him to the door and held his hand. He leaned forward to kiss her again and she offered her cheek.

"I don't believe you for a moment," she said.

She walked him to the bus stop dressed in an army jacket and a cotton smock that she called her second-grade art teacher's dress. She seemed very innocent, but falling in love with her would be very painful. Sydney was right; he didn't need that kind of pain at his age. He plucked a horse-chestnut blossom from a tree at the bus stop. "*Aesculus hippocastanum,*" he said, and handed her the flower as the bus pulled up.

"How did you know that?" she asked. "You think I'm a haughty bitch, don't you?" she said as the doors hissed shut.

When he returned to his apartment, he poured himself a Scotch and sat in the darkness in his leather pedestal chair, watching the traffic stream along the Outer Drive. He was tired. He was so tired of all the intricacy. "Anna T. Boffo—Sore Throat" was not a great line, even though she insisted. It lacked the cadence of a truly great line. Yes, she did look slightly orange in the corridor light. So what? He was turning yellow as he grew older. He was turning a parchment yellow. That much he knew. Yes, he did think she was a haughty bitch, That much he also knew. He sat in the darkness and sipped his Scotch and thought about calling her. The only light in the room came from the soft glow of the phone. He picked it up and dialed Information and asked for her number. He waited and fought to hold the number inside his head and then, just as it was about to fade, he called her.

"Hello?"

"Hello, this is Arthur Fabricant."

"Arthur, I didn't think I'd hear from you again."

"I'm home. I'm just sitting here."

"Arthur, I think we can be friends."

"Yes, I think so."

"Listen, Arthur, there's this really weird documentary on El Salvador at the Sandburg tomorrow night. Would you like to see it with me?"

He didn't answer her for a moment. "Yes," he said, and held the phone away and closed his eyes.

A Woman in Warsaw

H E WAS IN WARSAW for the International Book Fair. He'd never been in Warsaw before and he stayed at the Hotel Victoria and on his last night, after dinner downstairs, he went up to the Casino and had a brandy at the bar. A woman immediately moved over and sat beside him. She was quite beautiful, about 28, with gray eyes, very thin, with long brown hair, and dark stockings, dressed in a suit, like a young business woman.

"I am tired of the Germans here at the bar," she said in perfect English. "You're not German; I heard you speaking English."

"No, I'm American."

"Good. I like Americans."

He was a divorced man of 48 who owned a small academic publishing company in Baltimore. He had the face of a scholar with a high forehead, and gray hair, thinning and long at the back of his neck. He felt too tired to talk to her. He'd read in the International Herald Tribune of the death yesterday of Isaac Bashevis Singer. If she was a prostitute, he didn't want to get involved with her. On his last night in Warsaw, he only wanted to drink his brandy and then perhaps find a cab and take it to Krochmalna Street, the street where Singer lived in Warsaw as a young boy. He'd promised himself that before he left he'd go to Singer's Krochmalna Street and to the Warsaw Ghetto monument. He had to be in London tomorrow afternoon.

Then he surprised himself by saying to her, "I'll buy you a drink, but I'm leaving."

"Americans are always in a hurry. Where are you going?"

"To visit friends."

"You have friends in Warsaw?"

He nodded.

"I'll have a vodka." She called to the bartender who brought over a bottle of Wyborowa. She drank down the shot and looked at the man defiantly and brushed her hair back as it fell across her face. "Are you a Jew?"

"Why do you ask?"

She spread her pale fingers next to his on the bar. "See how dark your fingers are beside mine. Most of the Americans who come here to the hotel are Jews. They come to walk on the ashes. Have you come to walk on the ashes?"

"What business is it of yours?"

"It is my business. We have a large industry in ashes." She looked at him again. "I will take you to see the Ghetto in a Mercedes."

"I'm not interested."

"Not interested in what? I do not believe you. You do not look like a man who is not interested. Her gray eyes were very beautiful. She reached to the top of her hair and pulled her dark glasses down and lit a cigarette. As she bent her head down he noticed that her hair was really auburn colored, and as she leaned toward him, it brushed against his cheek. He wanted to reach out and touch her hair, but instead he got up and put two 50,000 zloty notes on the bar.

"You will leave me here with these foolish German tourists?"

"Perhaps I'll see you later." Then he touched the back of his fingers to her hair and then to her cheek. It was a consciously gentle gesture, but she angrily moved her face away from him and turned her back to him.

Outside the hotel he walked across the street to the plaza with the Tomb of the Unknown Soldier and stood with some people watching two young guards goose-step in cadence before the tomb. He stared at the soldiers' high-boned Slavic faces and their tri-crowned hats with chin straps, white gloves, and gleaming black boots. There was no sound other than the hollow cadence of their marching. He watched them for another minute, then turned away from them and found a cab.

He could speak a few words of Polish, enough to give simple directions. "Krochmalna Street," he told the driver. The word for street was 'ulica'... "Ulica Krochmalna." It was an old cab and the driver was a middle-aged man with thick glasses. He drove in silence for only five or six blocks and pointed to a building on the corner. There was a sign on the side of the building, Krochmalna Street. He got out of the cab and asked the driver to wait for him.

The Warsaw Ghetto had been destroyed by the Germans in 1943. Every building was burned. Before World War I Singer's father, a rabbi, brought his young family from a small town in the provinces to Warsaw and they lived on Krochmalna Street. As he walked along Krochmalna street he saw only apartment buildings with dark courtyards, a few with strands of wash hanging over the balconies in the courtyards. A family was sitting on a front stoop of a building. There were two blonde children, with tiny, inquisi-tive, fragile faces, sitting with their parents who quickly glanced up at him. He nodded to them and slowly walked back to the cab as they watched him. Before he got in he touched the bricks of the corner building.

He didn't know the word for monument. "Ghetto Monument," he said. The driver seemed to understand and touched his hat. He turned on his lights and drove to the Ghetto Monument. When they arrived, after a few blocks, the driver parked the cab under some trees at the curb, dimmed his lights and lit a cigarette.

There was a large park where he got out, and he immediately saw the silhouette of the Ghetto Monument. He approached from the rear, down a long walk. The monument was in a clearing of several city blocks, surrounded by apartment buildings.

Supposedly it would be the only monument in Warsaw without flowers strewn at its base. Someone at the Book Fair had told him that all the saints and cardinals and Polish military heroes would have flowers on their monuments, but the Ghetto Monument would be barren. There had been an old woman in front of the hotel selling flowers. He could have bought her last bouquet. She held it up to him as he passed her, but he shook his head.

He walked around to the front of the statue. There were some flowers lying at its base, a sheaf of dried red flowers. He picked up one, a red flower with a black throat, and put it on the arm of the figure of the man who was prostrate, lying with his head on his arm. Then he stood back with his hands clasped in front of him and bowed his head and tried to say a prayer in Hebrew. He knew only a few words of the Kaddish, the mourner's prayer. He looked up at the faces of the statue, a young man, bare chested, his coat thrown open, holding a grenade, and a young woman behind him holding a rifle. The commander of the Ghetto forces in 1943 was Mordechai Anielewicz, who was only 23. This was probably Anielewicz. He bowed his head and said what he knew of the Kaddish prayer. When he finished he saw someone in the distance walking at the edge of the park. A man passing on the sidewalk had noticed him and from afar lifted his hat to him in a gesture of respect.

He could then have asked the driver to take him to the Umschlagplatz, but he didn't. He didn't want to see it. The Umschlagplatz, the collection point in German, was the courtyard where the Germans forced the Jews to assemble before they led them to the trains. It wasn't necessary to see it, even though he'd been told that there was now a plaque there. Instead he told the driver to take him back to the hotel.

When they arrived the driver wanted to change money with him, and when he wouldn't change money, the driver was annoyed. Everyone in this country wanted to change zlotys for dollars. Soldiers, Boy Scouts, taxi drivers, the hotel maids. He just wanted to be left alone. He wasn't a money changer. He didn't acknowledge the doorman in the bearskin hat and gold-braided greatcoat, who solemnly held the cab door open. He ignored the doorman's assistance. He pushed into the lobby with its groups of tourists standing at the front desk and at the cashiers' cages. There were also some Polish officers and their wives, a few Russian officers in uniforms with red sideboards, and young Arab men reading and drinking coffee. He'd heard that the PLO trained guerillas in Czechoslovakia and that many of the Arab men in Warsaw were on leave from these camps. There was one fat older man in long robes who sat with them. He wore a fez, a monocle, and was reading a newspaper printed in Arabic.

He walked through the lobby and waited for the elevator to the casino bar. Up in the bar he ordered a brandy and drank it quickly. It burned as it went down and he ordered another and drank it just as quickly. Then he saw her getting up from a booth in the back of the room and walking toward him. She seemed to be covered with a green color, a soft, unusual, ancient green patina.

"Hello, American," she said. "Are you through with your communion?" She had eyes like a gray cat, and the tawny, sinister movements of a cat. "You see? I have waited for you. I knew you would be back. They all come back in about thirty minutes. Where are you from? Philadelphia? Boston?" She snapped her fingers at the bartender.

"Baltimore."

"Baltimore? I've never heard of it. Wladyslaw, I will have another Wyborowa, but over ice. How did you like the Ghetto? Did you go by Mercedes? There is nothing left to see there in the Ghetto. There is no Ghetto. Did you go to Mila Street?"

He signaled for another brandy. "No, I didn't know there was a Mila Street."

"Yes, of course, it was their headquarters there. Your countryman wrote a book, about it, what was his name...?"

"Leon Uris."

"Yes, Uris. Are you surprised I know of him? Of course I do. Jewish writers are very popular in Poland. Woody Allen. I know of him. We all love him. Even Jerzy Kosinski. He came back here only recently. It is a pity he committed suicide. Are you surprised that I know of American literature and films? Do you know I am a student at Warsaw University? Yes, a student of English literature. I come here occasionally, and if I see a man I like who will pay my price... I may go with him. Otherwise I just drink and read my book and go home alone. Did you ask me my price?" She shook her hair out at him. "My price is 1 million zlotys. What is it for you, a hundred dollars? Nothing. A meal or two. I can live on that for two months. And never have to come here. We will order a bottle of champagne and go to your room. Are you staying at the hotel?"

"I'm not interested in making love."

"Ah, love. Is that what you call it? I am not talking about love. We can discuss literature. What is your name?"

"Mark."

"Mark? That is not a Jewish name. That is the name of one of our saints, St. Mark. We have the name Marek."

"No, my name is Mark. What's your name?"

"My name? I never tell my name. Every time I have a different name. Tonight I shall also be a saint, St. Magdalena. Madga. She was also a whore. Our Lord Jesus was a Jew and he forgave her. Maria Magda. He blessed her as a saint and she washed his feet and dried them with her hair." She raised her glass. "Cheers, Marek. Drink your brandy."

He took the third brandy and now he was calm. The green that had colored her face was gone and he saw that she was dressed in black, almost like a young nun in her dark suit and immaculate white silk blouse. He remembered the young nuns as a child in Baltimore in the streets near his home, passing them on the sidewalk, their slim, high-planed faces, the ivory faces of the nuns as they passed murmuring in their black robes, the rustle of the hidden legs under the long robes.

"I'll go with you," he said. "Why not?"

"Good. We will buy a bottle of champagne and we will discuss literature." She snapped her fingers again at the barman. "Wladyslaw, champagne." She smiled at him for the first time. He reached out to her and with the same consciously gentle gesture touched her hair with the back of his hand, and then her face. This time she didn't turn away. He had always wanted to touch one of the ivory faces hidden behind the coifs and so now he determined he would do this and they would go together to his room.

"Before we leave, you must pay me my fee. Do you have dollars? I would prefer to be paid in dollars."

He had five $100 bills folded inside of a pocket in his checkbook. He removed the bills and handed her one. She looked at it quickly, opened it up and turned it over, and then opened her purse, put it in her wallet, and snapped her purse shut. She got off her stool. "Okay, let's go."

"I think I'll take another brandy to the room in a paper cup."

"How many brandies have you had?"

"Three or four."

"Wladyslaw, give the gentleman another brandy. Send it to his room. They won't allow you to take a paper cup through the lobby. Not even a glass. They're very decorous here. Did I say that right? I have difficulty with certain words."

"Yes, you said it right."

Up in the room, she put the bottle of champagne in the small refrigerator, removing most of the bottles of beer and wine the hotel had provided. He sat in a chair and watched as she moved around the room touching different articles. She went into the bathroom and came out with some plastic bottles of shampoo and lotion. "May I have these?"

"Yes."

She swept them into her purse. "And this?" She was holding a bar of milled French soap. She sniffed it and held it under his nose.

"Take it."

"Good. I can sell these things, you know, or keep them. I really don't need them. I prefer to sell them. How about this?" She held up a small sewing kit.

"Keep it."

"Thank you."

There was a knock on the door. "They're here already with your brandy."

He signed the check and gave the waiter a dollar. She went back into the bathroom and opened the champagne. He heard the pop. She returned with a face towel around the bottle and poured two glasses. "There is a telephone in there!" she said. "That's really decadent. That's something new. In Poland people have nothing, and the guests here now have telephones in their bathrooms. How do you explain that?"

"That's capitalism."

"If that's capitalism, I don't want it."

"Well, you don't have to use the telephone."

She sat on the bed and raised her glass to him. "Na zdrowie, that's how we say cheers in Polish." She crossed her legs and then began swinging her leg. She leaned over to a panel at the side of the bed and turned down the lights. He reached out to her and in the half darkness traced the contours of her face with his index finger, and then her lips.

"Okay, we'll talk of literature," he said to her. "Do you know of the writer Isaac Bashevis Singer? He died yesterday in the States."

"No, I didn't know that. He was a very sweet man, Singer. He wrote the novel 'Shosha'. Do you think I look like Shosha? I have her color of red hair."

He moved away from her and stood up and looked out the window. "I see Warsaw has a Coca Cola sign. It's the only sign I see."

"Yes, it's another gift from America. Coca Cola and a telephone in the bathroom. Just what we need." She shook up the bottle of champagne until it fizzed, and sprayed some of the champagne at the ceiling and then at him.

"You shouldn't do that."

"Why are you so quiet and sad, Marek? Is it because of Singer's death or your visit to the Ghetto, or are you drunk?"

He had difficulty focusing on her after four brandies. "I may be a little drunk."

"Are you a married man, Marek?"

"No, I was married."

"Where is your wife?"

"My wife? I have no wife."

She pushed another button for the radio at the night table. "Do you like Chopin? In Poland you can't escape him."

"Leave it on."

"Do you want to stay at the window? Why don't you sit on the bed?"

"Do you think Mary Magdalene really washed Christ's feet and dried them with her hair?"

"Is that what you want me to do for you? I won't do it."

"No, I don't want that."

"What do you want?"

"Do you know how to sew?"

"Sew? Yes, of course. Do you want me to give you the sewing kit back?"

"No, I want you to sew something for me. I don't know how to sew." He finished the brandy and sat down on the bed with her. "Did you take all the pens too?"

"Yes, pens and the letter sheets and envelopes. But I will give them back, and the sewing kit." She turned on the light and sat on the bed, and poured out the contents of her purse. Two plastic pens fell out with the sewing kit, several plastic bottles, the bar of soap, her wallet, a leather folio of stationery, and a letter opener and shears.

"You can have it all back, except for my wallet."

"No, you keep everything I just want to borrow a pen and the scissors from the stationery kit."

He began to draw a crude triangle on the yellow bedspread. He outlined a triangle, then bisected it with another triangle. He drew the design of the Star of David and then slowly lettered the word JUDE onto the center of the star. He took the scissors and cut the yellow star out of the bedspread. She watched him, sitting cross-legged, sipping champagne from the bottle. "You'll have to pay them," she finally said to him when he finished cutting out the star. "They won't allow this."

"I won't pay them. I don't care about their rules of decorum. I've already paid them."

"Now what?" She looked at him. She really was beautiful. Very inviting, very beautiful, with perfect Slavic eyes and cheek bones. She didn't look like Shosha though. He doubted if she was a student at the University. She was probably just a beautiful Polish hotel whore who liked to read. Although, maybe he was wrong, she could be a graduate student in literature. She knew too much about literature for her own good, and it disturbed him to have her as his seamstress. She was too intelligent. Now he just wanted her to leave. Maybe she was with the Polish version of the KGB, but what would they want from him? His book of photographs of the Warsaw Ghetto that he bought yesterday? "Getto Warszawskie"? Photos of Jews begging, skeletal children, hollow-eyed, dying in the streets?

He went to the closet and got his navy blue blazer and put it down in front of her on the bed. "Can you sew this star on my jacket? Right there?" He pointed to the breast pocket.

"Sew it?"

"Yes, right there. Sew this and you can go. You'll make Poland's last Jew. While you're doing that, I think I'll go into the bathroom and phone God and tell him what I'm doing. Use good strong basting stitches."

He went to the bathroom and ran water over his fingers and touched his face, and looked at himself in the mirror. She was right, he did look like a Jew. He spread his fingers in a fan in front of the mirror. He did have dark fingers.

"You're sewing?"

"Yes, be quiet. I haven't done this in a long time. You are a bit crazy, you know."

"And so are you."

"Yes, we are a good pair, a Catholic whore, Maria Magdalena, and a Jewish saint, St. Marek from Baltimore."

"I don't know who you are, but I'm not a Jewish saint."

"Did you telephone to God?"

"Yes, I did."

"What did you ask him"?"

"I asked him why three million Jews died here."

"And what did he say?"

"He said he didn't know."

"Do you accept that answer?"

"No."

"There." She held the jacket out and showed it to him with the star sewn on the breast pocket. "It's done."

"You're sure that it will hold? The stitches are strong?"

"Yes, of course. My grandmother taught me that cross-stitch. I call it Basia's stitch. It is done. It will last."

"Thank you very much. You may go now. Take the sewing kit, take the pens, all the bottles. Take everything."

She swept all the articles back into her purse. "You will be all right, Marek? Where will you go with that star on your jacket?" She looked at herself in the mirror and patted her hair. He could see that she had finished with him. She wasn't really interested in him, and in a minute would disappear forever.

"I don't know where I'll go."

She took a bottle of cologne from her purse and sprayed her wrists and throat. "I will leave you now, Marek, okay?"

"Yes, and take the bottle of champagne."

"I cannot believe you have given me a million zlotys for sewing, Marek. Only from an American. Someday, when I come to America, I will look you up." She opened the door, put her purse over her shoulder, and carried her shoes in her hand. She looked at him. "Ciao," she said, and instead of taking the elevator, she was suddenly gone, down the stairway.

He put the jacket on. She'd done a good job. He touched the star on his pocket and smoothed the hair at his temples, and caught the empty elevator downstairs. No one was in the lobby, no one paid attention to him as he passed. One man in front of the hotel stared at him and then quickly turned away.

He walked over to the plaza where the two young guards were still marching in cadence, and watched them. There were torches burning and a small crowd. No one noticed him, and he watched for a few moments and then moved to a park bench and sat down in the shadows of the trees.

If he'd had a portable phone with him, he could have called God again, but he wasn't in America so he didn't have a portable phone. If he'd had one, he could have set it on redial. He didn't have one, though, and he folded his arms around himself and sat quietly at the rim of the torchlight. He looked at his fingers. He did have dark fingers, even in the torchlight.

Suddenly she came up to him out of the shadows.

"Why are you sitting here, Marek? I saw you leaving the hotel."

He didn't answer her.

"You know, it won't do any good for you to sit here with your star, Marek."

She reached out to him and touched his cheek with almost the same gesture he'd used. "I'm going for my tram now. You really shouldn't stay here. Someone may hurt you. Do you understand that? You should go back to your hotel."

He watched her turn and slowly walk away from him towards the plaza. She turned back once more and called out to him, "You shouldn't stay there, Marek. It is dangerous for you to sit there." She stood looking at him for a moment and then shrugged and walked toward the shadows of the torchlight and she was gone.

About the Author

Lowell B. Komie is a Chicago attorney and writer. He received his B.A. from the University of Michigan in 1951 and his J.D. from Northwestern University in 1954. *The Judge's Chambers*, his book of short stories, was the first collection of fiction published by the American Bar Association. He is a contributing editor of *Student Lawyer*, the magazine of the law student division of the American Bar Association, where many of his stories have appeared. His stories have also been published in *Harper's*, *Chicago Magazine*, *Chicago Tribune Magazine*, *Milwaukee Journal Magazine*, *Chicago Bar Record*, *Canadian Lawyer* and other magazines and university and literary quarterlies. He was articles editor of the *Chicago Bar Record* in 1992 and 1993. He and his wife, Helen, live in Northfield, Illinois.

SWORDFISH
CHICAGO

Swordfish/Chicago

When my father, who died several years ago, wrestled with me or hugged me and held me in his powerful grip, the only way he would release me would be if I said our secret password, "Swordfish." He was a powerful, athletic man, a very graceful athlete, and he could have held me for an eternity, and I wish he had, but the secret password, "Swordfish," was always honored between us not as a sign of weakness, but as a matter of honor between father and son. So Swordfish/Chicago is named after my father. My mother would be very happy.

My father was a friend of the Marx Brothers when they lived on the South Side of Chicago. His particular friend was Zeppo, who he called Buster. On Saturdays the Marx Brothers, who raised pigeons in a coop on the roof of their boarding house, would take the pigeons to Calumet City and sell them to immigrants, who baked pigeon pies. Then Buster, Chico, Harpo and Groucho would rush back to the South Side, and my father would wait with them on their roof for the birds to come flying back. If you let the pigeons out of your grasp for a second, they would be off—and would fly back to the coop because they were homing pigeons. So the Marx Brothers sold the same pigeons each Saturday, over and over again. My father swore this is a true story.

Years later, I learned that the Marx Brothers made a movie in which all through the movie the secret password was "Swordfish." So I finally learned where my father got the name, and I pass it on with these stories to you.